I0553896

Erotic Encounters
Volume One

by

Samantha Gentry

Erotic Encounters Volume One

Contact Information: info@thewildrosepress.com

Cover Art by *Diana Carlile*

The Wild Rose Press, Inc.
PO Box 708
Adams Basin, NY 14410-0708

Visit us at www.thewilderroses.com

Publishing History
First Scarlet Rose Edition, January 2014
Print ISBN 978-1-62830-139-7
Digital ISBN 978-1-62830-140-3

Published in the United States of America

Unexpected Encounter

Chapter One

Dane Wingate scrutinized Shasta Brooks' short auburn hair, beautiful green eyes and a body even her tailored slacks and blazer couldn't hide. She handled the business transaction for the obviously confused elderly woman with a patience and compassion that touched the vulnerability he tried to keep safely tucked away. Life had taught him that such a liability was one to keep hidden, not an asset to let anyone else see.

He sucked in a deep breath, held it for a moment, then slowly exhaled. No matter how attracted he was to her, he didn't have time in his life for any type of personal involvement, not until—

"Next."

Shasta's voice jolted him from his thoughts. He flashed his patented sexy smile as he sauntered toward her window, trying his best to appear casual and confident. "Good afternoon, beautiful. How's my favorite bank teller today?"

She returned his smile with a dazzling one of her own. "I can say in all honesty, I'm glad it's Friday. The bank will be closing in a few minutes, and I'm not working a Saturday morning shift this week."

"Sounds like you have big plans for the weekend." He winked at her as he shoved a check across the counter. "I'd like to cash this."

She looked at the check. "You know, it would be

much quicker for you to use the ATM if the only thing you want is cash from your account."

"I know, but the ATM is so impersonal. I'm very big on the *personal* touch." Using the bank's ATM would certainly have been much quicker, but it wouldn't have allowed him to hear her sexy voice or see her beautiful smile.

Over the past few months, ever since the bank became one of his clients for his computer consulting services, he had steadily grown in lust with her. It had slowly dawned on him over the last month that perhaps more than just the physical attraction captivated him. How much more and exactly what that *more* consisted of he didn't know and unfortunately couldn't allow himself the indulgence of finding out. At least not until he had his life straightened out and could once again do as he pleased.

He leaned forward slightly, inhaling deeply to take in the scent of her perfume. "Is that a new fragrance you're wearing?"

"Yes. It's called *Surrender To Passion*." Her eyes sparkled, and her tone took on a teasing quality. "Do you like it?"

He lowered his voice to a husky whisper. "Sounds like words to live by." He tilted his head to one side and raised a questioning eyebrow. "Is that the philosophy you follow?"

The heat of embarrassment spread across Shasta's face, a flush she knew tinged her cheeks a vibrant pink. Without a doubt, the man had the sexiest smile and voice she had ever encountered. And his eyes...they weren't just blue. They were the most incredible shade of turquoise. She had never seen eyes that color. They fit perfectly with his sandy blond hair, handsomely chiseled features, broad shoulders and athletic build. And when you put it all together, it added up to the most desirable and sexy man she had ever met.

She forced a calm to the surge of sexual tension and heated need that spoke to her whenever she saw him. Spoke to her? What an understatement. It required a concentrated effort to keep from leaping across the counter, ripping off his clothes and indulging the numerous fantasies that flooded her mind whenever she thought about Dane Wingate.

She counted out two hundred dollars, then smiled as he picked up the bills. "Is there anything else I can do for you today, Mr. Wingate?" *Anything...anything at all. And I do mean anything.*

"How many times do I need to tell you? It's Dane. And in answer to your question," a sly grin tugged at the corners of his mouth, "I'm sure there's several things you could do for me." He glanced at his watch. A bit of a scowl wrinkled across his forehead. "Oops, I didn't realize it was so late. I barely made it here before closing time. I'm definitely behind schedule."

A hint of disappointment squelched her mounting desires and ongoing hope every time he came into the bank. Would this be the day he asked her out? Perhaps an elegant dinner followed by a very special dessert. "Have a nice weekend, Mr. Wingate...I mean, Dane."

"You, too, Shasta." He winked at her again as he pocketed the cash, then headed for the front door. He glanced back and gave her a parting smile before leaving the bank.

She watched his retreating form for a moment. The dampness seeped into the crotch of her panties, and her nipples tightened against her lacy bra. Just the sight of Dane Wingate left her horny as hell. She had fantasized on more than one occasion about his naked body and the marvelous things she would like to do to it. And then there were all the exciting things he could do for her.

But beneath the heated desires that consumed her whenever she saw him buzzed an undercurrent wanting to know the real person behind the sexy grin and smooth voice—the man himself. What type of books did he read? What kind of movies did he like? What type of music did he listen to? Did he have any brothers or sisters? Had he ever been married? She wanted to know everything about him.

The only thing she knew was the information on his account at the bank—thirty-two years old and not currently married. A hint of a frown crossed her forehead. At least she assumed he was single. He didn't wear a wedding ring, and his was the only signature on the account.

She took a calming breath, glanced at the clock and watched as the branch manager locked the door, signaling the close of business. She hurried to balance her cash drawer, then drove straight home.

After retrieving her mail from the front porch mailbox, she sorted through the envelopes as she walked down the hall to her bedroom. Tomorrow was her thirtieth birthday. On one hand, she looked forward to the party the girls at the bank had planned for tomorrow night. On the other hand, it seemed to her that thirty should be some kind of a milestone signifying some sort of life accomplishment.

She had a good job as head teller at the bank and

was in line for promotion to assistant branch manager. But her personal life remained steeped in a daily routine that lacked the type of excitement and spontaneity she longed for. She couldn't even find an exciting lover to occupy her time with earth shattering hot sex, let alone the loving committed relationship she wanted.

She had been engaged briefly during her senior year of college, more as something she thought she was supposed to do rather than true love. Fortunately, she had discovered in time that her fiancé only wanted someone to bask adoringly in his glory rather than an independent woman with thoughts and an identity of her own. It had turned out to be a disaster she didn't want to repeat.

Even though she still secretly yearned for a lifetime commitment with that one very special man, she had adopted the outer appearance of a dedicated career woman on her way up the ladder of success. Her vibrator offered more satisfaction than her most recent attempt at a relationship and had proven vastly more dependable.

After stripping down to just her panties, she pulled on her favorite old worn jeans and a cotton T-shirt. Her best friend, Gillian, was bringing the pizza and a movie while she provided the bottle of wine. Just another quiet night at home. She pursed her lips in a moment of contemplation. There had been too many quiet nights at home lately.

Somewhere in the greater Seattle metropolitan area, there had to be a sexy man who had eyes only for her, a man who would respect her independence and could make a commitment to a lifetime relationship. Someone with a sense of humor. Someone who could carry on an intelligent conversation on a variety of topics. A caring and compassionate man she could give her heart to and know he would treat it with respect and tenderness.

And when the lights were turned down low, a man who could fuck her into a state of blissful exhaustion.

A heavy sigh of resignation escaped into the air. Was she doomed to continue on the present course? The strong career woman who spent lonely nights at home? The doorbell interrupted her moment of reflection.

"Surprise!" A chorus of voices greeted her when she opened the door. Her genuine laughter followed a moment of stunned silence. She stepped aside to admit her female co-workers from the bank, each one carrying a birthday present. Gillian and Trudy had boxes of pizza and several bottles of chilled champagne.

Shasta shook her head as she beamed at her friend. "I can't believe this, Gillian. You had me completely fooled."

"That was the plan. The best way to pull off a surprise party is to make you think there's a party planned for the next night. We've got food and drink, although I'm not too sure if pizza and champagne really go together."

"Champagne goes with everything," Trudy called from the kitchen as she set the pizza boxes on the counter.

"And we have another surprise for later," Gillian added.

"Another surprise?" Shasta cocked her head to one side. "What is it?" She couldn't stop the grin tugging at the corners of her mouth. "Come on, tell me. Don't leave me in suspense!"

A knowing smile spread across Gillian's face. "No, no, no. Then it wouldn't be a surprise. I can only say you'll definitely love it."

Gillian opened bottles of champagne and filled glasses while Trudy dished up the pizza. Music filled the house, competing with the voices and laughter for control of the noise level. As the hour grew later, Gillian called for everyone's attention.

"It's time for the birthday girl to open her presents." Shasta sat in the chair indicated by Gillian as the presents were stacked on the table next to her. Giggles and laughter filled the room as she unwrapped one risqué gift after another until each present had been opened and passed around for everyone to see.

A warm sensation flowed through Shasta, a combination of champagne and good fun. "I see the presents have a definite theme. I can honestly say I haven't seen such an interesting collection of naughtiness anywhere other than a catalogue featuring adult toys and sexy lingerie. Thank you one and all." She tried unsuccessfully to suppress a grin. "I hope to put all of them to good use."

Appreciative laughter greeted her comment as she quickly ran her gaze over the various items again. Crotchless panties, clip-on nipple rings, massage oils, chocolate body paint, edible thong underwear with a different flavor for each day of the week, three different types of vibrators, including a vibrating butt plug, Ben-Wa balls, a deck of Kama Sutra playing cards and a book of erotic photographs.

Several enticing images flashed through her mind. Dane's head between her legs as he nibbled at the cinnamon-flavored thong, a vision so real she could almost feel his warm breath on the sensitive skin of her inner thighs. Dane reclining on her bed while she painted his erection with the chocolate body paint, then slowly licked it off. She pictured herself sitting astride his body, his cock buried deep inside her pussy with the nipple rings teasing his lips when she rocked forward. Her breathing quickened to match the throbbing need coursing through her veins.

Gillian's ringing cell phone brought Shasta's attention back to reality. She attempted to bring her raging hormones under control by taking another sip of champagne, but it didn't help.

Gillian quickly disconnected from the call. "Can I have everyone's attention? I know some of you have to work tomorrow morning, but we have one final surprise for our birthday girl before the evening comes to a close. Standing on the porch right now is the hottest male stripper in Seattle who has stopped by to give Shasta a very special birthday present. Ladies…" She nodded to Trudy who opened the front door. "I give you the one and only, the Macho Marauder in the flesh. And what delicious looking flesh it is, too."

Six-feet one-inch of tanned skin covering hard muscle stepped through the door and into the living room. Dark, shoulder-length hair framed a face hidden behind a mask. Tight black pants hugged his long legs, stretched across a perfectly rounded ass and accentuated an impressive bulge at his crotch. Broad shoulders and the hard planes of a bare chest supported the flowing black cape. The entire package oozed pure sex. Orgasmic electricity crackled in the air.

He glanced around the room at the assembled

women, each wearing a look of anticipation. Then his gaze fell on Shasta.

She didn't know which shock was greater, the one she felt or the one she saw in his eyes. The dark hair didn't belong, but there was no mistaking those mesmerizing turquoise eyes and that devastatingly sexy smile. Her fantasies paled in comparison to the reality that dominated her living room in the person of Dane Wingate.

Shasta forced herself up from the chair, slightly unsteady on her feet from a combination of champagne and shock. She held out her hand toward him. "Now, this is the type of birthday present a girl can truly appreciate. It's a pleasure to meet you…Mr. Macho Marauder."

He took her hand and brought it to his lips, then he reached into the pocket of his cape and produced a rose. After giving a courtly bow, he handed it to her. "A lovely flower for a *very* lovely lady."

"Thank you." She felt more like a tongue-tied school girl than a sophisticated career woman. Her entire body tingled with anticipation. Her nipples hardened into taut buds of arousal and pushed against the soft fabric of her T-shirt.

Gillian turned on the pre-arranged music, and the Macho Marauder went into his act. With a dramatic flip of his wrist, he twirled the cape from his body and let it drop to the floor.

Shasta managed to stifle her gasp. Not even in her wildest fantasies had she visualized such a perfect body cloaked in an overwhelming sexual aura. Each pelvic thrust reached out to her, beckoning her to get out of the chair and join him.

She squirmed uncomfortably as she fought the pull of his magnetic presence. Her pussy muscles clenched when his black leather pants disappeared in a flourish. Hard muscled thighs, an intriguing tattoo and a black leather thong that barely held an impressive cock in place. The nearly naked man gyrating in time to the music had her heart pounding with the same rhythm.

Forcing her attention away from his body, she made eye contact with him. His gaze remained riveted on her, the glow of passion simmering in the depth of his eyes. It felt as if he truly danced only for her, oblivious to everyone and everything else in the room.

She couldn't break the mesmerizing hold he had on her. The only thing she seemed to have under her control, at least for the moment, was her ability to remain in her chair. And that became more difficult with each passing second.

The bumps and grinds, the near nakedness in a room of panting women, did not bother Dane. He had become nearly oblivious to a sea of hard nipples in the audience. He had etched out a comfort zone that allowed him to perform without getting physically aroused. Being turned on to the point of ending up with an erection was not a problem for him the way it was for some of the other male strippers at the club. At least that's the way it had been until tonight.

To his dismay, the control he prided himself on had slipped away. When he had been hired for a private performance at a birthday party, it had never occurred to him that Shasta Brooks would be the recipient of his attentions. She looked adorable in her faded jeans, T-shirt and bare feet, so different from the properly tailored business clothes she wore at work. And the more he watched her—the excitement covering her face, her nipples puckered against her T-shirt, the soft fabric caressing her full breasts—the more turned on he became.

If he didn't wrap up his performance in the next minute or two, he ran the risk of his cock wiggling its way out of his thong and leaping toward her. And the last thing he wanted to do was embarrass Shasta. He forced his gaze away from her, taking a minute to glance around the room. Performing had never turned him on the way he was at that moment.

He couldn't afford the luxury of becoming personally involved with someone, not until he had his life straightened out so that it was his own again. Now that she knew, what did she think about his night job? Was she disappointed? Or perhaps disapproving? For some inexplicable reason, her opinion mattered to him. He cleared the disturbing thoughts from his mind and concentrated on finishing his performance.

Fifteen minutes after his arrival, his clothing lay strewn about the floor, and he wore only a thong cradling his cock in supple black leather.

Trudy was the first of the guests to head toward the front door. She made an exaggerated show of fanning herself. "Damn…it's very hot in here. I've got to hurry home. My husband is in for the thrill of his life. And if I can't wake him, my vibrator may end up blowing a circuit!"

The others voiced their agreement and quickly followed, each wishing Shasta a happy birthday before hurrying out the front door. Only Gillian remained behind. As Shasta carried empty champagne glasses to the kitchen, Dane picked up the bits and pieces of his costume and shoved them into a small duffle bag. He left the dark wig and his mask in place. Pulling out a pair of sweat pants, he slipped them on as he prepared to leave.

"A very impressive performance." Gillian held out a check toward him as she blatantly stared at his crotch. "Very impressive, indeed." She tried to slip the check inside the waist band of his sweat pants, but he deftly avoided her attempt and took it from her hand.

"Thank you. It was my pleasure." He shoved the check into his bag. "Now, if you'll excuse me, I'll say good-bye to the birthday girl." He flashed his sexy smile, gave Gillian a wink, then walked into the kitchen.

Dane shot a quick glance behind him to make sure Gillian stayed in the living room rather than following him. Then he turned his attention to Shasta. "Well…this is a bit awkward." He kept his voice low so only she could hear him. "The look on your face when I arrived made it obvious my wig and mask didn't keep you from recognizing me." He nervously glanced at the floor, then regained eye contact with her. "Thank you for not exposing my true identity."

"I was as surprised to see you as you obviously were to see me." An amused chuckle escaped her throat. "And as far as *exposing* you…well, you did a marvelous job of that yourself. And all this time you've led me to believe you're a computer consultant. I must say," she blatantly looked him up and down, "you don't look anything like a stereotypical computer geek."

"It's my day job. You know that. The bank is one of my clients. I'm good with computers and have a degree in computer science. It's always come easy for me. This," he gestured toward the mask and wig, "is my night job."

"Obviously, Gillian didn't tell you the birthday girl's name."

Dane shot another quick glance in Gillian's direction to make sure she was still occupied in the living room. "Would it be okay if I came back after your friend leaves? I want to explain this to you. I don't want you to misunderstand."

"You don't owe me any explanations."

"I may not owe you an explanation, but I'd like to give you one. Please?" He was thankful for the mask that hid the uneasiness he felt.

"How about in an hour?"

A feeling of relief settled inside him. "Perfect. I'll be back in an hour."

Shasta walked him across the living room. When they reached the door, the Macho Marauder took her hand in his, brought it to his lips and gave a courtly bow. "Happy birthday, lovely lady." Then he left.

A quick side glance picked up the curious look on Gillian's face, but Shasta chose to ignore it. She had far more interesting things on her mind at the moment. Her skin tingled where his lips had touched the back of her hand.

Flopping onto the couch, she let out a long, low whistle. "That is the most gorgeous hunk of man I've ever seen."

Gillian's soft chuckle quickly turned into a wickedly sexy laugh. "Jeez, that's got to be the biggest understatement of the century." She licked her lips as she picked up the jar of chocolate body paint. "Wouldn't you love to impale yourself on that cock after licking off this yummy chocolate? Hot sex and tasty chocolate…what a perfect combination. Talk about a fuck to die for." She emitted an exaggerated sigh and set the jar on the table. "Yep, I could go to my grave a happy woman."

Gillian visibly composed herself as she glanced around the living room at the party aftermath. "I'll help you clean this mess, then I guess I'll make the trek home to my empty apartment. Maybe I'll plug in Mr. Vibrator and see if he can satisfy this twitch the Macho Marauder created."

Shasta laughed as she gave her friend a hug. "You and every other woman who was here tonight. Thanks for the surprise party. This is the best birthday I've ever had. Don't worry about this mess. I'll tackle it in the morning." She ran her gaze over the array of gifts on the table. "As soon as I get rid of you, I might just try out some of my new toys."

Gillian's laugh joined Shasta's. "Personally, I'd much rather try out the Macho Marauder."

"Well, one has to make do with what one has." Shasta glanced at the clock. *And in forty-five minutes I'll have the Macho Marauder all to myself. Happy Birthday to me!*

As soon as the door clicked shut behind Gillian, a wave of anxiety washed over Shasta. She looked around the living room at the party remains. Suddenly, the full impact of her agreement to let Dane return hit her in force. Fantasizing about sizzling sex with him was one thing, but reality quite another. What had she done? Had it been the champagne talking?

As long as the situation wasn't real, she had easily entertained a myriad of erotic thoughts about Dane

Wingate. But did she have the nerve to act on her fantasy when faced with it in the flesh? And would her desire for more than a quick roll in the hay with this incredibly sexy man lead her to expect more from him than a one night stand?

The earlier buzz from the champagne had worn off. Maybe another glass would prop up her dwindling courage and slow down her rapidly growing anxiety. She shook her head at the surprising turn of events. Dane Wingate...a male stripper. Never in her wildest imagination would she have guessed that one.

And judging by the way her friends had behaved, he could have had his pick of any of them, even the married ones. That was probably the way things were for him every night when he performed at the male strip club. He obviously had women constantly throwing themselves at him, providing him with all the sex he could ever want. So why did he ask to return after everyone had gone? He said he wanted to explain something, but why would he feel he needed to? And why specifically to her?

That thought continued to nag at her consciousness. Was it nothing more than a ploy to add her to his list of conquests? One more notch on his bedpost? She experienced a moment of sadness. Could her dream man possibly be that shallow and self-absorbed?

A slight frown wrinkled her forehead as another thought made itself known. If that was the case, why hadn't he ever asked her out? She had openly flirted with him just as much as he had flirted with her. Surely he must have known she would accept his invitation to dinner. Definitely a puzzling situation.

She poured herself a glass of champagne, hoping it would help dull her disappointment at the thought of him considering her nothing more than a quick fuck for the night—do a sexy strip, get her juices flowing, then cash in on his investment of time and energy. Was that standard procedure for him whenever he performed at private birthday parties? One of the fringe benefits? Bang the birthday girl before calling it a night?

She drank deeply from the glass. It might not dull her disappointment, but it certainly made her feel fuzzy all over...warm and fuzzy. Or was the heat the result of the knowledge that Dane Wingate would soon be back in her living room? Just the two of them all alone.

Shasta picked up the book of erotic photographs and leafed through the pages as she finished the glass of champagne. She squirmed uncomfortably in the chair as her mind substituted the image of his face and nearly naked body for each of the men pictured in the book. Her pussy throbbed with need. Her bare nipples puckered against the soft fabric of her T-shirt, creating a sensual feel that added to her growing arousal.

In a moment of champagne fueled impulsiveness, she pulled up the front of her T-shirt, fastened the clip-on nipple rings, then pulled her shirt down again. She cupped the underside of her breasts through the fabric and jiggled them, causing the nipple rings to pluck at the tautly puckered buds. She couldn't decide if the odd sensation excited her senses or merely pinched.

She grabbed the opened bottle of champagne and emptied the remaining couple of swallows into her glass. As she brought the glass to her lips, the doorbell rang. Her heart skipped a beat before pounding with a strange combination of excitement, anticipation...and trepidation. The nipple rings teased her senses while stimulating her awareness of the tantalizing sensation.

One unsteady step toward the door brought her to a quick halt when the full impact of the champagne hit her. *Holy shit! I'm swacked. I can't let him know.* She wrinkled her forehead into a frown. *Think sober. Think sober.*

Sucking in several deep breaths, she held each one for a moment before exhaling. One foot in front of the other, one step at a time, she carefully made her way across the living room. She paused at the door long enough to take another deep breath before opening it.

Shasta didn't know if she felt relief or disappointment when she saw him fully dressed in jeans and a pullover shirt. The long black wig and the mask were gone, the bare chest covered. She reached out a slightly trembling hand and touched the front of his shirt, feeling the hard planes of his chest beneath the fabric. She didn't know what to say but couldn't stop the nervous giggle. Then the words just seemed to slip out on their own. "You didn't need to get dressed on my account."

The dangerously sexy smile she had come to appreciate showed a row of perfect white teeth. "To tell you truthfully, all that stuff I wear when performing is uncomfortable—especially that damn wig."

"Then why do you wear it?" She motioned him inside, then shut the door.

His expression became serious. "As I said, I want to explain. I don't want you to harbor any wrong assumptions about what's going on or what I'm all about. I'm basically a straight forward simple down-to-earth type of guy, in spite of what you've discovered tonight."

The sound of her spontaneous laughter filled the room. "*Simple down-to-earth type of guy* is not exactly the description I'd use for the Macho Marauder—a man whose job is to take his clothes off as entertainment for a room full of screaming horny women."

Oh, no. Did I really say horny? I've got to get my mouth under control. No more champagne for me. Bad birthday girl. Bad birthday girl.

He took her hand and led her to the couch. There was no mistaking the surge of desire that shot through her the moment she felt his touch. Even in her slightly impaired condition, she knew it was caused by more than the champagne.

"That's what I wanted to explain." Dane sat next to her. He had never been in such close proximity to her for this long. She had a natural beauty that gnawed at his vulnerability.

He brushed his fingertips across a cheek that felt as creamy smooth as it looked. The sensation of her skin against his sent a wave of desire crashing through him.

Surrender To Passion...the fragrance still clung to her skin, tickling his senses, enticing him with forbidden thoughts. He wanted to give her his undivided personal attention again and again and again until the wee hours of the morning when they were both too exhausted to move, then do it all over again.

He had long ago learned to turn his mind off when he did the Macho Marauder strip act. And as far as putting his nearly naked body on display...well, it was just skin. No big deal. Self-consciousness about body image was not a hang-up for him. Everyone had a body, with each person's being different and unique unto itself.

But performing for Shasta. That had been very personal compared to the other private performances he had been hired to do. Every time he saw her, he wanted to have her naked in his bed. Just watching her excited him. Her eyes glowed with a hidden desire as her breathing quickened. Her tongue occasionally darted out, licking her slightly parted lips.

"The wig...the mask...by making them part of my act, I get to remain anonymous. I don't want my *extra-curricular* activity intruding into my normal business routine. I don't want any of my clients recognizing me at the club. I can go about my daily business without concerns of whether my nighttime alter ego will have a negative impact on my career."

"Then why do you do it?" She furrowed her brow in momentary confusion. "Does having a secret kinky side spice up your life?"

Dane's muscles tensed. He resisted the initial reaction to pull back from the sting of her words. Did he really come across that way? As some ego driven jerk?

Shasta reached out and gently touched his arm. "I...I'm sorry. I didn't mean that the way it sounded. I have no business making judgments about your personal life. It's just that it was such a shock. It's not the type of thing I would have associated with a computer consultant."

She withdrew her touch from his arm, then rubbed her fingers against her temples, drew in a deep breath and held it a moment. "I think I had one too many glasses of birthday champagne."

Settling his fingers beneath her chin, he lifted until

they had eye contact. He delved into the depths of her eyes as he studied her. He offered a gentle smile, hoping to convey that he wasn't unhappy or insulted.

"I have a feeling my explanation is going to be wasted on you tonight." He leaned his face close to hers and placed a tender kiss on her forehead, then emitted a sigh of resignation that contained a touch of disappointment. "Perhaps it would be better if I left so you could get some sleep."

She shook her head. "Uh...no. I'm fine...really. I don't usually drink this much and especially not champagne. It was all the birthday festivities...uh...I'll make some coffee."

"I think some fresh air might be a better idea." Dane stood up and held out his hand toward her. "Come on," he extended his most sincere smile, "we'll take a walk around the block. Then if you still want some coffee, I'll make it."

After a moment's hesitation, she placed her hand in his. "We can take that walk if you'd like, but please don't feel you need to sober me up. I'm fine." She flashed a warm smile. "Honest."

Dane clasped her hand in his, resulting in a hard jolt of lust. Even though he had learned to disassociate his physical desires from his Macho Marauder performances, he still didn't have a whole lot of control over the aftereffects that told him he was every bit as horny as the women who watched him and tried to pull at his clothes while he performed.

Mindless sex with strangers was not his style. But Shasta Brooks represented far more than the concept of relief for an aching cock, a fast fuck or a one night stand. He tried to shove away the need pulling at him.

He was very selective in the women he became physically involved with, a result of needing to keep his club performances decisively separate from his personal life.

Before things went any further, he wanted to explain himself to her. He wanted to make sure she understood that he wasn't a tomcat constantly on the prowl for fresh pussy and using a male strip club to find it.

Chapter Two

"Let's take that walk anyway." Dane offered Shasta an encouraging smile. "While we're getting that fresh air, I'll explain the Macho Marauder to you."

"Wait." She looked down at her bare feet. "My shoes..." She wiggled her feet into a pair of canvas slip-ons, then shoved her house key in her pocket. "I guess I'm ready."

He laced their fingers together. Her hand felt so good in his, as if it belonged there. They walked along the sidewalk in silence for a couple of minutes as he tried to collect his thoughts about how to explain things to her and exactly how much of his past to reveal. And even more confusing were his thoughts about why he wanted to explain something so very private and personal, something he had never confided to anyone.

"About my Macho Marauder alter ego...it has to do with money. Stripping provides the maximum amount of money for the least amount of time and effort while not interfering with my real career. I've worked hard to establish my computer consulting business. I don't want to jeopardize that, but I need all the extra cash I can get my hands on as quickly as possible so that I can...uh, pay off some heavy bills."

An uncomfortable ripple of anxiety invaded his consciousness. The last thing he wanted to do was reveal any details of his dysfunctional family background. He had spent most of his adult life trying to disassociate himself from anything and everything family related. "For medical expenses."

"Medical expenses?" She stopped walking, bringing him to an abrupt halt, her alarm obvious. "Are you ill?"

"No, not at all. I'm in excellent health. I don't even catch colds." They started walking again as he collected his thoughts. How to explain without really revealing things he had tried so hard to bury deep inside him? "The expenses were incurred because of a lengthy illness my mother had before she died three years ago. I've been working to pay off that debt. A few more months and the Macho Marauder can fold his cape, throw away his mask and disappear into the night never to be seen again." He chuckled as a thought occurred to him. "And get rid of that itchy damn wig."

"You've been doing this to pay off your mother's medical expenses? Are you doing this on your own without any outside help? What about your father? Other family members? What about insurance?" A moment of alarm crossed her face followed by a hint of embarrassment. "I'm sorry. That's obviously none of my business."

How to explain without really explaining…how to answer her questions without really answering them. "There was some insurance but not anywhere near enough. I wasn't legally responsible for her medical bills, but I was the only one around to take care of her so it kind of fell to me by default. I guess you could say I felt an ethical obligation to settle her debts, and a male strip club provided the path to the maximum amount of money in the shortest amount of time for the least amount of effort." He tightened his hold on her hand in an attempt to get closer without seeming to be pushing her.

"I came up with the mask and wig as part of my act, and everything just seemed to fall into place. I had no idea the Macho Marauder would become such a big hit. In fact, he's been so successful that I'm going to be able to settle the entire debt a year sooner than I originally thought." *And then I can start to think about a personal life again.*

The street lights provided just enough illumination for Shasta to see the faraway look in his eyes, one that told her he had given her all the explanation he intended to. It left her wondering why he hadn't mentioned his father or any siblings and why his voice held a hard edge when saying he was the only one around to take care of his mother. It was obviously a very private matter for him—private and painful. Something he didn't intend to discuss.

And something she knew was none of her business.

A soft warmth spread through her body and touched her heart. This sexy man whose physical presence had been driving her crazy for several months had turned out to be quite a surprise in more ways than one. First as a male stripper exuding hot sex, then as an honorable man striving to do the right thing even though it would have been much easier to walk away. A very powerful combination—raw sexual magnetism and personal integrity.

They walked for several blocks while engaging in casual conversation, eventually arriving back at her house. He had proved to be even more fascinating than she originally thought. He knew exactly who he was and what he wanted, a man able to live comfortably with his own reality. He presented a commanding physical presence even without the Macho Marauder's costume.

There was so much more she wanted to know about him. But right now she wanted a night of unbridled passion with the sexiest man alive. The nipple rings created erotic little twinges, arousing her desires even more than they already were. She had given a quick thought to removing them but decided to immerse herself in the provocative new sensation they provided.

Back at her house, she headed for the kitchen. "I'll make that coffee now."

He grabbed her arm and stopped her in the dining room before she reached the kitchen door. "Don't go to the trouble on my account. How are you feeling?"

"I'm fine. That walk in the fresh air is just what I needed." She flashed a smile, half appreciative and half embarrassed. "I must apologize. Champagne makes me act…well, it does strange things to me. The party and…"

Dane laced their fingers together, tugging gently until he had her enfolded in his arms. Her breasts pressed against his chest, her tautly puckered nipples obvious even through both of their shirts. And the nipple rings she had not been wearing when he did his act, the ones he couldn't help but notice among the birthday gifts on the table, were now blatantly obvious as they adorned her breasts.

With one arm banded around her back, he threaded the fingers of his other hand through the soft strands of her auburn hair. A moment of uncertainty made him pause. If he had asked her out to dinner, a legitimate date separate from his stripper job, then he would welcome this opportunity to be with her. To revel in the anticipation of what the night could bring and proceed with confidence. But the circumstances left him uncertain. Perhaps if he…

Shasta took the decision away from him. She slipped her arms around his neck and lifted her mouth to his. Her actions, neither tentative nor unsure, caught him off guard, but only for a second. He shoved aside his concerns and captured her mouth with a kiss that demanded everything of her and promised as much in return.

She tasted of champagne and pizza, a strange yet intriguing combination. He flicked his tongue across her lower lip, then invaded her mouth with a heated passion that left no question about his desires or where they were headed.

He caressed her shoulders and back, finally running his hands across her perfectly rounded rear end. He snuggled her hips against his. A tightness pulled across his chest as his arousal grew. Even through her jeans, he felt the heat radiating from her body.

One hand on her ass, he slipped the other inside the back of her T-shirt. Her creamy skin tantalized his fingers and teased his senses. His cock twitched with a life of its own, wanting to find a hot nest to call home.

A hint of concern tried to force its way back into his consciousness. Taking advantage of a woman who had a bit too much to drink was not his style. He wanted a partner as hot and turned on as he was, someone whose desires matched his own, someone fully aware of what she was doing and the choices available to her, not a woman merely complying with what she thought he wanted.

His conscience told him to back off and give her a clear cut choice, offer her the option of putting a stop to things before they got totally out of hand. But logic won out. He wasn't forcing her into anything. If she wanted him to back off, all she had to do was say so.

He parted her lips with his tongue and probed the inside of her mouth. Her taste, the texture of her tongue against his, it all meshed together in a sensual twining that emulated the prelude to a sultry mating ritual.

She slipped her arms around his neck as she pressed her body against his growing erection. Her enthusiastic response presented all the encouragement he needed and helped dispel his concern about taking advantage of her. If her actions were a measure, she desired him as much as he did her.

The blood raced hot and fast through his veins. His breathing became labored. No other woman had ever turned him on so quickly. He wanted her, all of her, in every way possible.

But before his mind totally shut down, a disturbing thought forced its way in. Surely she must have reservations about what went on at a male strip club, about the reality of horny women throwing themselves at the performers. About how many strangers he had fucked in quick one night stands. It was a thought he couldn't dismiss and one he needed to address before any clothes came off.

Dane held her at arm's length. He pulled in a steadying breath as he tried to calm his rattled nerves. He had to get his rampaging desires under control but could not bring himself to completely turn her loose. In the three years he had worked as a male stripper, this was the first time he had been with a woman who knew about his night job—about his alter ego.

"There's something else I think you should know, something I'm sure has crossed your mind. Women at the strip club...I don't indulge—"

"Shh." She placed her fingertips against his lips. "We can talk later."

His last remnant of control flew out the window. His final attempt to first and foremost be a gentleman deserted him. He scooped her up in his arms. "Which way to your bedroom?"

He carried her down the hall to the room she indicated. Rather than placing her on the bed, he lowered her feet to the floor in front of him. A light brush of his fingertips across her smooth cheek sent a tiny shiver racing across the surface of his skin. One hand went up her back beneath her T-shirt, and the other cupped her perfectly rounded ass.

"You are," his words turned to a husky whisper, "without a doubt, the most beautiful woman I've ever seen."

The front of his jeans strained against the pressure of a hard cock demanding its freedom. He inched her T-shirt up, revealing her bare breasts capped with the clip-on nipple rings he had seen earlier among her birthday gifts. A moment later her shirt fell to the floor.

As he reached for the waist of her jeans, he felt her fingers tug at his zipper. He gently brushed her hand away. "Not yet." He unfastened her pants and slowly inched them down her hips and legs until they rested around her ankles. She stepped out of them without hesitation, kicked them aside and stood before him wearing only panties.

"I want to know every inch of your body, drink in your essence." With slightly trembling hands, he lowered her panties. As he deposited them on top of her jeans, she reclined in the middle of the bed.

Dane's chest heaved with his labored breathing as he gazed down at Shasta's naked body stretched out enticingly. The clip-on nipple rings dangled from the tautly puckered buds that capped her full breasts. "I want to feel my cock buried deep inside your delicious looking pussy...again and again and again."

Heated desire had him out of his clothes in a matter of seconds. His rigid shaft stood tall and thick, clearly defining his arousal and total readiness.

Her response said it all. She extended an inviting smile as she reached out and wrapped her hand around the girth of his hard shaft. A deep growl of need clawed its way out of his throat accompanied by a quick pelvic thrust.

"Shasta..." He couldn't force any more words out of his mouth. The way she gently stroked the length of his cock set his nerve endings on fire, threatening to consume him in a blaze of sexual frenzy and have him coming much too soon. He wanted to give her at least two orgasms before he even considered his own needs.

She opened her legs, inviting him into her most intimate recess. His stare became riveted to the soft auburn curls covering her mound, her erect little clit showing through, and her delicate pussy lips glistening with moisture. His breath caught in his lungs, and for a moment, time seemed to stand still.

He managed to physically pull away from the sensation of her fingers skimming along the underside of his stiff cock and took in a steadying breath. Every cell in his body, every place of consciousness in his mind, told him something very profound was about to happen. Something that exceeded the pleasures of hot sex. Something much deeper. Something far more personal.

Passion burned in the depths of her eyes, a heated desire that matched his own spark for spark. He wanted so much to please her, to take the fervor he saw beckoning him and turn it into rapture and fulfillment.

He snuggled his waist tightly against the curls covering her mound, the moisture seeping from her body onto his skin. He flicked the tip of his tongue back and forth across one of the clip-on nipple rings. Her soft moan of delight excited his senses. Tugging on the ring with his teeth, he managed to remove it. After placing it on the nightstand, he took her pebbled nipple into his mouth.

Suckling gently at first, the action quickly turned into a demanding hunger for more. He allowed her hard nipple to pop out of his mouth. The wet bud sparkled in the light like an exquisite jewel as her breasts rose and fell with her ragged breathing. He pulled off the other nipple ring and with a slightly trembling hand placed it on the nightstand next to the first one.

The mere touch of his bare skin against hers proved far more exciting than she had anticipated. A sultry purr escaped her throat when he scratched his fingers through the curls guarding the entrance to her pussy. Her head sank back into the pillow, followed by a sensual moan when he inserted his finger between her quivering folds.

Her skin tingled and her nerve endings danced in

delight as he licked and kissed his way down her body, all the while stroking his finger in and out of her wet sex. She squeezed her vaginal muscles around his finger to let him know she wanted more. He immediately obliged by inserting a second finger and using his thumb to massage her clit.

Just as she had imagined the scene a couple of hours earlier, Shasta looked down and saw his head between her legs. His hot breath tickled against the sensitive skin of her inner thighs, sending tremors through her body. Only instead of nibbling on the edible thong underwear, his lips plucked at her engorged clit. Her hips jerked upward, shoving her sex against his mouth. He quickly removed his fingers and replaced them with his tongue.

Soft moans escalated to whimpers of desire in response to the way he aggressively thrust his tongue between her pussy lips several times, pausing with each insertion long enough to tease the walls of her tunnel before withdrawing and invading again. Her ever increasing levels of excitement produced jerky and erratic movements as she rushed toward the ultimate rapture. He wrapped his lips around her clit. It only took a couple of sucking motions before she exploded in what she knew was the first of many delicious orgasms she would experience before the night was over.

Wave after wave of intense euphoria crashed through her body as his mouth continued to devour her, his lips tugging and sucking on her sensitive clit. She grabbed her breasts, squeezing and kneading the firm flesh. Her head thrashed back and forth against the pillow. No doubt about it...Dane Wingate's mouth should be classified as a lethal weapon of pleasure. He had already far surpassed every fantasy she had ever entertained about him.

Before her body could come down from the heights of her orgasm, his continued ministrations to her highly sensitive clit drove her right back up and over the top again. Her words rushed out in a breathless whisper as she gasped, "Oh, my God…more. That's the most incredible…"

She thrust her pelvis hard against his mouth, holding his head between her legs as she ran her fingers through his thick hair.

It was as if her words unlocked the last of his restraint. A deep growl, a combination of primal need and pure lust, escaped into the air. It reverberated against her pussy sending tremors of nerve-tingling vibrations rushing through her body. She wanted his cock, to touch it, to taste it.

Using her hands, she tried to maneuver him into a different position, but his mouth seemed to be fused to her honey pot. "I want…give me your cock…I need…"

Her words finally penetrated his single-minded pursuit of catering to her pleasure. Dane raised his head from her steaming sex and sucked in a couple of deep breaths. "What can I do to please you? What would you like?"

"I'd like for you to stay all night." *Holy shit! Did I really say that out loud? He has me totally out of control. I want more…much more.*

His gaze traveled up her body from behind the wet curls matted against her mound. He flicked the tip of his tongue against her stiffly engorged clit, eliciting a quick intake of breath from her. "Yes, I would like that very much."

Her heart continued to pound as she slowly regained her breath. It was a much needed break from the intensity of the orgasm spiraling inside her. This would be, without question, the best birthday she would ever have. Nothing could top this night of unbridled passion with a man who had dominated her fantasies so many times.

A quick expression darted across his face as she scooted her body away from him. She flashed a wickedly sexy grin. "I'll try to erase that look of disappointment. Turn over on your back and let me please you as much as you've pleasured me."

The twinkle in his eyes said her words had been what he wanted to hear. Then a hint of a frown wrinkled his forehead. "Before we get carried away even more than we already have, I need to get some condoms from my jeans—"

"There's some in the nightstand." She opened the drawer and pulled out several packets.

"Ah, yes…I like a woman who's prepared."

He quickly complied with her instructions by stretching out on his back. His rigid cock stood at attention, the head a reddish-purple. She licked her lips in anticipation of the tempting treat. The length and girth of his shaft were not only impressive, she found the shape and definition truly beautiful to look at. She gently cradled his balls, then bent to kiss the tip of his cock. Her entire body surged with sexual energy, her pussy still tingling from the thorough inspection his talented mouth had performed.

She laved the rounded head with the flat of her tongue, then proceeded along the underside until she reached his balls. His quickened breathing and low rumbling groans told her he liked her efforts and wanted more. She drew just the head into her mouth, held it there for a moment, then gradually sucked in more and more of his length. She felt each of his engorged veins as his cock filled her mouth. Her lips formed a tight seal around the girth.

She continued to suck, working the muscles of her mouth up and down the length of his shaft. And all the while she cradled his balls. His hip thrusts conveyed his appreciation. She hummed softly in response. His cock felt so good in her mouth, the intensity of the moment almost overwhelming her grip on reality.

To her surprise, he pulled her off, lifted her hips and turned her around so that she stretched out on top of him. The moment his warm breath fluttered across the damp curls covering her mound, her vaginal muscles contracted, as if trying to find something to grab hold of. She wrapped her arms around his hips and fondled his balls while once again taking his rigid shaft into her mouth.

Dane wasn't sure how long he could last. Her mouth...her hands...the feel of her body stretched out on top of him. His every nerve ending jumped and twitched with excitement as it responded to her talented ministrations. Her taste filled his senses with everything he knew it would be...and much more. The nectar of the gods, a spice uniquely Shasta. His mouth filled with a taste he knew could easily become an addiction.

Spend the night. Yes, that was exactly what he wanted to do. To make love to this fantastic woman again and again. He already knew this was much more than sex, more than the concept of being able to shove his cock into a hot pussy.

His chest heaved as his labored breathing turned ragged. He flicked his tongue across her clit before sucking it into his mouth. Her body convulsed into another orgasm as she ground her honey pot against his lips. He kneaded the globes of her ass cheeks, the feel of her firm flesh as exciting as everything else about her. She let out a low moan of pure pleasure as her muscles contracted and tugged at his tongue. She was everything he had ever desired.

Waves of ecstasy crashed through Shasta's body. No one had ever so thoroughly ministered to her with just his lips and tongue, and no one else's cock had ever felt so perfect in her mouth. She didn't want the night to ever end.

"If you don't ease up on my cock, you'll waste this perfectly good hard-on before I can finish making love to you." His words floated toward her, sounding as if he barely had enough breath to get them out.

She allowed his shaft to slip from her mouth, closing her lips around just the head for a moment before letting go and moving off Dane's body. He reached for one of the condom packets and ripped it open.

"Let me." She rolled the condom onto his rock-hard cock, her motions as jerky as the erratic breath she pulled into her lungs. When she finished, she fondled his balls for a second and then placed a tender kiss on each one. She leaned back into the softness of the bed and beckoned him with her smile. His turquoise eyes, clouded with smoky passion, told her of his intense arousal. She parted her legs, welcoming him into the intimacy of her pleasure core.

Dane supported his upper torso with his arms so he could watch her beautiful face as he entered her. Inch by inch, he slowly penetrated the moist heat of her tunnel. Her inner walls enclosed his rigid shaft in a tight sheath. He trembled as the power of the moment overwhelmed him. He wrapped his arms around her head and buried his face in her hair to keep from blurting out words he didn't dare say.

He had fucked more than his share of women since he lost his virginity at the age of fifteen to an older and experienced woman of seventeen. Screwing just for the sake of drowning in hot sex. But no way could that describe his coupling with Shasta. They were making love with a passion he had never before encountered.

Moving in and out with long sure strokes, he set a smooth rhythm, each thrust reaching to the depths. She wrapped her legs around his waist, her hips arching to meet each of his down strokes. They moved in perfect harmony, as if they were long time lovers totally in tune with each other's most primal needs and desires.

As much as he wanted to prolong every delicious moment, he couldn't stop the rush from churning in his balls, signaling his approaching release. He pumped faster, his strokes becoming harder and shorter. One more orgasm, if he could just hold on long enough for her to have one more.

Then she cried out. Her muscles contracted sharply around his shaft, and convulsions once again claimed her. His tenuous hold on his control evaporated. One last deep thrust. He held her tightly in his arms as the hard spasms of white hot release shuddered through him.

As the waves subsided, neither of them spoke.

They stayed wrapped in each other's embrace until their breathing slowly returned to normal. He raised up on one elbow just enough to be able to see her face, not wanting to withdraw from the perfection of her incredible velvet-lined muff. The sheen of perspiration dotted her flushed cheeks and forehead. Her green eyes glowed with a contentment that literally touched his heart. He smoothed loose tendrils of hair from her damp skin.

"You are so beautiful. You absolutely take my breath away." He placed a tender kiss on her lips. "What is it that would please you?"

Shasta looked up into the ardor of his gaze, a passion that touched every fiber of her existence. "I can't think of anything that would make this moment more perfect."

Except maybe knowing that we could have some kind of a future together.

The thought had popped into her head unbidden and not exactly welcome. What happened? She had never allowed her emotions to get away from her like that. They had known each other only as business acquaintances, despite their flirting banter and her secret longings. Then tonight, her world suddenly exploded into a frenzy of heated desire, hot sex and satiated needs. Not exactly the type of thing to base a relationship on or judge the possibility of a future.

"Neither can I." He continued to hold her tightly. She could actually feel the beating of his heart, the pulsing of his life. It was a phenomenon she didn't want to ever lose. He cradled her head tenderly against his shoulder and kissed her cheek then carefully rolled off of her. "Don't go anywhere. I'll be right back."

Shasta watched Dane disappear into the bathroom. She closed her eyes as a smile curled the corners of her mouth. Her mind wandered to what the rest of the night would bring and for that matter, where things between them were going.

His weight settled into the bed, bringing her thoughts back to the present. She opened her eyes, but the sight that greeted her was not what she expected. His expression showed an uncertainty, a level of apprehension.

Or was it just her imagination? Could she be projecting her own fears and concerns about where the night and their relationship was headed onto the moment?

A tremor of anxiety shivered inside her as she softly touched his cheek. He captured her hand in his and brought it to his lips, kissing her palm. A fleeting gesture of intimacy, but the physical contact warmed her heart and soul. As absurd as it sounded, she wondered if she could actually be falling in love with this man who seemed so open and honest on one hand, yet retained an air of mystery and hidden secrets on the other.

An uncomfortable embarrassment settled over her. She felt pressured to say something to break the silence and cover up her nervousness and the sudden surge of trepidation. "There's some cold pizza left in the kitchen, along with some champagne. Are you hungry? I could stick the pizza in the microwave and heat it up if that would make it more tempting for you."

"Being here with you is all the temptation I can handle." He brushed a tender kiss across her lips, then allowed a warm smile. "But I am kind of hungry."

Samantha Gentry

Shasta scooted toward the edge of the bed, but Dane tugged on her hand to bring her to a halt. His mind had been racing with unanswered questions and concerns. The last thing he wanted was to lose this incredible woman. Just hearing her voice, feeling the warmth of her skin, made his heart sing.

He delved into the emerald fathoms of her eyes, took a steadying breath and allowed the words to find their way into the open. "You asked me to stay the night. I'm asking you if I may stay the weekend. I don't want to leave when dawn arrives."

A shy smile lit up her face. "A fantasy weekend? I would like that very much."

He hadn't realized he'd been holding his breath, waiting for her answer, until he exhaled. He placed another soft kiss on her lips, gave her hand an intimate little squeeze and slid out of bed, pulling her along with him. He folded her into his embrace and just held her, swaying gently, savoring the sensation of her bare skin pressed along the length of his naked torso. His heart beat a little quicker as he inhaled the combination of her perfume and the lingering scent of hot sex. The stimulation caused his cock to twitch and jump. He wanted her again. He *needed* her again. Did he dare assume?

The last thing he wanted was for her to believe his only interest in her centered on how many times he could fuck her in one night. To have her think it was a contest of some sort among the male strippers at the club with the winner receiving the Golden Cock Award for stamina. For the first time, he wished he had been able to find another way to earn the money other than the strip club even though it would have taken much longer to pay off the medical expenses.

Dane tried to force the confusion from his mind. For someone normally very confident and in charge of what went on around him, he found himself wandering in the unfamiliar territory of uncertainty. Shasta Brooks had his reality turned sideways and upside down.

He reluctantly released her from his embrace but kept hold of her hand. He was comfortable in his own skin and didn't feel awkward or embarrassed being undressed in front of other people, even before he started performing at the strip club. In fact, it was one of the reasons he had originally considered stripping as an option to earn extra money. But that didn't mean Shasta felt the same.

Glancing around her bedroom, he spotted her robe on a chair. He picked it up and held it out toward her, but she took it from him and tossed it aside.

"A fantasy weekend calls for uninhibited behavior." *Oh wait. Will he think I'm an oversexed party girl who sleeps with any good-looking stud who happens to cross my path?* "Dane…I don't want you to think that this is…that I normally go to bed with—"

He brushed a quick kiss across her lips, effectively stopping her words. "I don't think any such thing."

He had already fulfilled the fantasy she had been carrying around inside her. No matter what he wanted, she knew she would willingly comply. Even though her pussy still tingled from the intensity of their lovemaking, a throbbing need for more of him made itself known.

"Fantasy weekend?" He grabbed the nipple rings from the top of the nightstand. The sexy smile that so mesmerized her every time she saw it slowly spread across his handsome face. "With that in mind, do you think I could talk you into putting these back on?"

She returned his smile with a sly one of her own. "I don't know. What do I get out of it?"

He leaned forward and used his tongue to tease one of her nipples into a tautly puckered bud. "You can have anything you want." His words tickled across her ear as he clipped one of the rings on her nipple.

The throbbing need pulsed between her legs as she took the other nipple ring from his hand. She thought of all the adult toys the girls had given her for her birthday. She certainly wouldn't be needing the Ben Wa balls this weekend to keep her in a state of arousal. With Dane Wingate standing naked in her bedroom, artificial stimulation was the last thing she needed.

She clipped on the other ring and impulsively shimmied her shoulders so that her breasts jiggled. The rings plucked at her taut buds, sending a rush of desire straight to her pussy.

A glow of passion lit his eyes as he watched her. Never in her life had she felt as totally free and uninhibited as she did at that moment. She joked with the girls at work about naked romps on the beach and hot sex, but it was mostly talk without the action to back it up. Her vibrator got most of her action. It worked as a momentary substitute to relieve the buildup of sexual tension, but it didn't keep her warm on cold nights and couldn't hold her in its arms and tenderly kiss away her moments of sadness.

His muscles flexed, and his body tensed. He swallowed as if trying to keep his composure. Trailing his fingertip across the rise of her breasts, he took her hand in his as he forced out the words. "If we don't head for the kitchen right now to find that cold pizza, we'll never get out of this bedroom."

She widened her eyes in feigned innocence. "And that would be a bad thing because..."

His spontaneous laugh filled the air. He tugged on her hand as he started for the bedroom door. "It's obvious that I'm going to need sustenance if I'm going to keep up with you, my sexy vixen."

They walked hand in hand to the kitchen. Shasta dished up four slices of pizza on a plate and put it into the microwave while Dane took a bottle of champagne from the refrigerator and opened it. He poured each of them a glass and held his up in the form of a toast.

"Here's to our fantasy weekend. May it be everything you want it to be. And may it be the first of many."

As they each took a sip, his words swirled around in her mind. *The first of many.* If only she could figure out how to make that more than just words.

Chapter Three

After finishing the last of the pizza, Shasta put things away in the kitchen. Dane offered to help, but she shooed him out of the way, saying it would be quicker if she did it herself. He took the opportunity to look around, ending up at the table where all her birthday gifts had been stacked. He gave a closer inspection to each item than his initial quick glance.

Though it was well after midnight, he turned out the living room lights so no one could see in when he opened the drapes and sliding glass door that led to the patio. To his surprise and delight, he spotted a hot tub. They would definitely be using it before their fantasy weekend came to an end.

He closed his eyes and allowed the sensations and memories to flow over him. The feel of her skin, the sound of her voice, the silky strands of her hair, the burning passion in the depths of her emerald eyes. She consumed all his thoughts.

The sex had been great. In fact, it had been a thousand times better than merely great. But there was so much beyond just sex. A fantasy weekend? The implication was a weekend spent indulging all the carnal pleasures. But he wanted more than that. He wanted to spend time getting to know her. What were her likes and dislikes? What about her family?

Family. He didn't want one. He didn't *need* one.

He had himself to depend on and that's all he needed. Lifetime relationships? A sham with no basis in reality. He had seen first-hand that no such thing existed. He would never be dependent on anyone and didn't want anyone to ever be dependent on him for anything other than business.

So what was he doing in Shasta Brooks' house, asking to stay the weekend and staring out across her patio wondering about the future? Exactly when had he lost control of his life? He shook his head. A stupid question. He knew the exact moment it had happened. It was when he had pulled her into his arms and kissed her for the first time. He knew deep down in his soul that his life would never again be the same. His life was no longer his own regardless of how much that thought scared him. At that instant, he had made the decision to share it with her. It hadn't even been a conscious thought, only a deeply intuitive moment of certainty.

But what to do about it? Give in and let it happen or fight the inevitable? And what about Shasta? What was it she wanted out of life? Did her career take priority over everything else or might there be room for him?

He fought to shove away the thoughts that were neither appropriate nor viable. He had no business even pondering what the future held until he finished paying off the medical bills. And even then, did he have what it took to be involved in a successful relationship? After all, look at his role models—totally dysfunctional parents who lived miserable existences.

He closed the patio door, pulled the drapes shut and wandered toward the kitchen. Too many questions and no answers. He watched Shasta put the last of the dishes into the dishwasher and start the washing cycle. His gaze traced the outline of her nude body—the curve of her hips, the uplifted breasts with the dangling nipple rings, the auburn curls covering her mound and decorating the entrance to paradise. And her beautiful face with the perfect mouth and emerald eyes.

To maintain mind over matter in order to keep his cock under control while performing was one thing, but that talent seemed to be failing him as he stood at her kitchen door. He couldn't stop the arousal and desire from engorging his veins so that his erection stood tall and hard. And he had no way of hiding it from her view.

Walking up behind her, he slipped his arms around her waist and kissed the back of her neck. "I see you have a hot tub. We should make use of it before the weekend is over." He forced himself to keep his hands at her waist instead of brushing his fingers down her abdomen and across her mound on the way to the moist entrance of her delicious sex. "I also took a look at your collection of birthday presents. Quite an array of adult toys. Do you have any whipped cream to go with the chocolate body paint? It would make a good substitute for a birthday cake tomorrow night."

She leaned back against his hard chest and closed her eyes as she placed her hands on top of his. He pressed his erection against the small of her back, savoring the physical contact.

"I don't have any whipped cream, but I can certainly find some by tomorrow night." Her voice dropped to a seductive whisper. "Is there anything else you can think of that we might need?"

He turned her around in his embrace so he could

see her face and look into her eyes. A hard jolt of emotion overcame him, stopping the words before he could get them out. He held her tighter, snuggling her bare body into his and cradling her head against his shoulder. It felt so right having her in his arms. He didn't want to let go. "Perhaps another day added to the weekend. Just Saturday and Sunday aren't going to be enough."

Is it possible to fall in love in one night?

A shiver of anxiety quickly followed his thought. He didn't know where it came from or exactly what it meant, but he did know that it scared the hell out of him. He found himself sinking farther and farther into an emotional abyss, and he didn't know how to get out.

Or if he even wanted to.

Shasta circled her arms around his waist and melted into the sensual warmth he projected. "We could make use of the hot tub right now if you'd like. If we leave all the lights off, no one will see us. We will need to keep our voices low so we don't wake the neighbors."

He placed a kiss on her cheek and whispered in her ear. "I can be quiet if you can."

She turned off all the lights inside the house then opened the drapes and sliding door to the patio. Together they stepped outside. The controls indicated the water was at the right temperature. Dane took the lid off the hot tub. Clouds of steam escaped into the cool night air.

They climbed into the bubbling water and settled next to each other on the underwater bench. The sensual feel of the water lapping against her skin increased her desire, and the answer to that desire was only a touch away. She slid her hand across his thigh. His muscles immediately tensed followed by a soft moan.

She leaned her head back and closed her eyes, allowing her hand to remain resting on his inner thigh. Just that little bit of physical contact, knowing that he was there, filled her with a sense of contentment. The swirling water soothed and relaxed her muscles. Comfort and contentment…as if everything she had ever wanted was finally within her reach.

"I want to know everything about you." His smooth voice penetrated her thoughts. He placed his hand on top of hers and enclosed it within his fingers.

They spoke quietly, sharing the sense of closeness. She talked about her work and hobbies, and he told her about his computer consulting business but didn't elaborate any more on the medical expenses he was working to pay off or his experiences at the male strip club.

He laced his fingers with hers. "Tell me about your family."

"My mother and father live in Montana, as does my brother along with my niece and nephew. I went to college here in Seattle and decided to stay after graduation."

"Have your mother and father enjoyed a long and happy marriage?"

She looked at him quizzically. "That's an odd question." She tried to formulate an answer to a question that left her uncomfortable. "Well…no. They've been divorced for fifteen years. My brother is also divorced." A hint of anxiety joined her discomfort. "I guess that's one reason why I haven't been all that anxious to get married and chose to concentrate on my career instead."

She normally didn't like giving out that much information about herself, but he was so easy to talk to. He listened attentively, making her feel as if what she had to say was very important to him. She found herself telling far more than she had ever revealed to anyone, even her closest friends. She even told him about her disastrous engagement. She bared her soul but truly felt as if she could trust him with the knowledge.

"How about you? Tell me about your family."

He hesitated a moment before answering her question. "There's really not much to tell."

She waited for him to continue, but he didn't say anything else. She allowed a moment of disappointment when he didn't confide the same depth of personal information to her. There was something in his past troubling him, something to do with his mother and father he didn't feel he could share. She reminded herself that it had only been a matter of a few hours since he had returned to her house following her surprise party. Though it felt as if she had known him for a long time, other than seeing each other at the bank, their relationship was still in its infancy. If it could even be called a relationship rather than an unexpected encounter resulting in hot sex.

Dane released her hand, put his arm around her shoulder and pulled her close. He placed a tender kiss on her lips that quickly escalated into the heated passion bubbling inside them in the same way the water bubbled in the hot tub. Sparks of incendiary desire. Spontaneous combustion that even the water couldn't douse. A hot flame that couldn't be quenched.

He thrust his tongue into her mouth, aggressively

seeking out the dark and tantalizing recesses. She responded by tickling her fingers up his inner thigh until she came to his rigid shaft, standing tall and ready for action. She wrapped her hand around its girth and slowly pumped. It had been a long time since she had sex in a hot tub. Her entire body tingled with excitement. She wanted…no, she *needed*…to be touched everywhere. She wanted to indulge every intimacy this sexy man could provide.

And as if reading her mind, his hands grasped her hips and placed her straddling his thighs and facing him. He spread his legs apart, leaving her balanced with her thighs on his. The hot water swirled around her breasts, teasing her nipples. She continued to stroke his hard cock as the underwater jets shot gushing streams against her pussy and ass suspended between his legs. The stimulation sent tremors of excitement coursing through her. Then the incredible sensation of his fingers replacing the jets of water pushed her to a higher level of arousal.

One of his hands in front and one in back, his fingers tempted and teased. He rubbed his thumb against her engorged clit as he thrust two fingers in and out of her pussy. She moaned softly as she leaned forward, shoving harder against his hand while at the same time thrusting her ass up.

He responded to her silent urging, pressing his fingertip against her puckered anus. A jolt of wicked pleasure rippled through her body at the prospect of this new experience. She wiggled her ass, pushing back against his touch. He answered by slowly inserting the tip of his finger into her anus. She flinched slightly, then a low growl of pure lust clawed its way up from deep inside, demanding more of this marvelous new sensation. He continued to stimulate her clit and pussy while at the same time working his finger farther in her tight and untried back door.

The rampaging sensations twisted around inside her like a tornado, growing stronger and more intense with each passing moment. "Oh, my God...that's unbelievably incredible."

"If you like this, then you're going to love what I have in mind for later."

"Ooh...is that a promise?" Before he could answer, she leaned forward and pressed her open mouth against his, aggressively seeking out the feel of his tongue.

Her mind tried to wrap around all the invading sensations, intensely powerful vibrations. Her chest heaved with each ragged breath she drew. His tongue twined and meshed with hers. Fingers stroked in and out of her pussy and probed her anus. Was this a limited version of what a ménage a trois felt like?

She had always been curious about that but never had the nerve to explore the possibility. Had never met a man she felt she could trust with the extreme intimacy of the first step—that of anal intercourse.

All thoughts stopped as orgasmic waves crashed through her body, touching every part of her reality. Her muffled cry of release filled his mouth, and then she slumped forward against his chest.

Her hand slipped away from his rigid shaft. The loss of her sensual touch, of the stimulation, caught Dane momentarily off guard. His chest rose and fell erratically as he tried to force his breathing back to normal. Tremors of need swept through him. He could not hold out much longer. Now that he had experienced the intense pleasure of her body, had tasted a touch of heaven, he knew he would always want to be with Shasta and only Shasta. And right now he wanted her out of the hot tub and into bed before he totally lost it and fucked her then and there without taking any precautions.

He wrapped his arms around her and held her close. "We've probably been in here too long. We need to get out of this hot water."

"You're right. There are towels in the cupboard behind you."

He wanted...he *needed*...her. He craved the sensation of her pussy muscles tugging and squeezing his shaft as he thrust to the depths of her tunnel. He hungered for the addictive taste that belonged to her alone. The feel of her creamy smooth skin against his, the pebbled texture of her tautly drawn nipples...

After reluctantly breaking the physical contact with her, Dane pulled out two large beach towels and wrapped one of them around Shasta as she stepped out of the water, then he wrapped the other around himself. He held her again, not wanting to release her yet knowing that they couldn't continue to stand on her patio dressed only in towels. He replaced the lid on the hot tub, and they went inside. As soon as she closed the door and drew the drapes, he switched on a table lamp.

Damp tendrils of auburn hair clung to her wet cheeks. Her skin appeared flushed, partly from the heat of the hot tub but also from her orgasm. He wrapped his arms around her. "You look tantalizingly delicious."

He pulled the towel from her body and used it to dry her. He talked to her while gently rubbing and patting her skin. "You are an incredibly exciting woman, and I've decided to let you have your way with me."

She made an exaggerated show of batting her eyelashes. "That's very tempting." She slipped her hand under his towel and stroked his obvious erection.

He grabbed her wrist and quickly stepped away from her enticing touch. "You keep doing that, and I'll be forced to back you up against the dining room wall and fuck you until you beg me for mercy." His voice teased even though the words had been uttered with a slightly breathless rasp to them. Once again the surge of desire rushed to his cock reaffirming his readiness.

And once again the sensual touch of her fingers skimmed along the underside of his rigid shaft. Her lips nibbled at his chest, telling him she was every bit as hot for him as he was for her. He grabbed several carefully selected items from her birthday gifts displayed on the dining room table and handed them to her. Her smile said as much as any words could. He scooped her up in his arms. As he had done just a few hours earlier, he carried her down the hall to her bedroom.

He placed her on the edge of the bed, then took the toys from her and set them on the nightstand. "Which of those do you want to play with first?"

"I think these would be fun." She held up a bottle of flavored massage oil and the vibrating butt plug.

He flashed a lewd grin. "I see you want to pick up where we left off. I like the way you think." He uncapped the bottle of oil. "Scoot over to the middle of the bed, turn on your stomach, pull your legs up under you and wiggle that beautiful little ass at me."

Shasta eagerly complied with his instructions, wanting more of the excitement he had given her in the hot tub. In fact, she knew exactly what she wanted and that she wouldn't be disappointed. How strange it was. With Dane, she felt totally uninhibited, not afraid to try new things or let him know exactly what she wanted. She had never trusted anyone as much as she did him.

He rubbed the oil into her butt cheeks, kneading her flesh with his fingers. She thrilled to his sensual touch. One thing about their sex play and lovemaking had become crystal clear. Dane Wingate was much more than the greatest lover she had ever experienced. He was also the most considerate. He seemed to really care about her needs and desires.

He penetrated her puckered hole with a well-lubricated finger, making sure she was comfortable with it before continuing. She jumped when he added a second finger. He immediately paused in his efforts, genuinely concerned. "Are you all right, Shasta?"

"Absolutely." Her voice had become a husky whisper. She shoved back against his hand and wiggled her ass to let him know he had not hurt her. He placed a tender kiss on each butt cheek as he worked his fingers, stretching and preparing her for something more substantial.

With his free hand, Dane reached around her hip and stimulated her engorged clit. Her throaty moan of pleasure combined with her ragged breathing to produce a sound that stiffened his cock even more while tugging at every sensual nerve ending he possessed.

Judging she was ready, he grabbed the butt plug and turned on the vibrating function to make sure it worked then turned it off.

Shasta heard the soft buzz. Her breathing

increased, and her pulse raced. Her entire body tingled with anticipation. With the exception of Dane's fingers, her ass was still virgin. The concept of anal intercourse had always frightened her a little, but not with Dane. She knew he would be gentle and patient. It would be a memorable experience to be repeated often with the right man.

And Dane Wingate was that man.

She glanced over her shoulder at his handsome face behind her. "This little toy can be the third person of our ménage a trois."

His grunt of appreciation accompanied by a sly grin and the smoky passion in the depths of his turquoise eyes told her how much he liked her suggestion.

"You've never done this before, have you?" His words came out as a husky rasp, attesting to his heightened state of arousal. "I'm playing with a virgin ass. Is that right?" He leaned forward and placed a soft kiss on her shoulder. "I only ask so I'll know how to proceed. The last thing I want to do is to cause you pain."

Her breathless words reflected her state of arousal. "Well…uh, it's true. This is my first experience."

"I'll try my best to make it memorable for you." He placed a string of kisses down her spine, then licked the raspberry massage oil from her ass cheeks and removed his fingers from her anus.

Dane poured a small portion of the oil into the palm of his hand and thoroughly lubricated the putt plug. After flicking on the vibrating function, he placed it against her rear opening. She jerked to attention.

"Just relax, honey. Don't tense up." He playfully

nipped at each of her ass cheeks with his lips. "Are you okay? I don't want to hurt you."

"More than okay." She purred her contentment.

"If you want me to stop, all you have to do is say so." He eased the tip of the butt plug into her puckered entrance.

She struggled to get the words out. "I've never felt...oh, God...anything like this. I can't even think straight...Dane..." Her words trailed off into soft moans.

His hard cock throbbed with his need for her touch, for the moist heat of her pussy and the way her muscles squeezed and stroked his length. But his needs would have to wait. He couldn't allow his churning passion to rush her as if this were an everyday occurrence.

He slowly pushed on the plug, pausing several times so she could accommodate the size and feel as it penetrated her body. Soft moans and sensual gasps, her sounds of sexual excitement fed his heightened arousal while also providing him a sense of contentment knowing he was giving her pleasure. When he finally had the plug fully inserted, he reached around her hips and gently massaged her stiff clit. She remained on her knees and elbows. Her ragged breathing turned into cries of delight, her words barely understandable.

"I want you...want your cock...your mouth...all of you...oh, God...that's incredible."

Shasta knew the vibrating butt plug would be different than anything she had experienced, but she had no idea just how different. Or how intensely exciting.

But she wanted more. Her pussy throbbed with need. Her muscles convulsed, looking for something to grab hold of. Her mind fogged as her ability to think faded, leaving only the torrid sensations coursing through her. She tried to wiggle out from under his body, and he backed away.

"I want to be on top." Before he could answer, she shoved him onto this back and straddled his chest. His stiff cock bobbed in front of her face, the head a deep purplish-red. She laved it with the flat of her tongue, the texture and action fueling her excitement. Then she took it into her mouth.

A moment later his arms wrapped around her hips and pulled her pussy down to his mouth. He nibbled at her clit with his lips and teased it with his tongue. He added to her pleasure by grasping the butt plug and sliding it in and out of her ass. All the intense sensations merged into one. The butt plug vibrated inside her. Her clit felt as if it would burst any moment. She took more of his length into her mouth.

Everything at once. So much. Almost too many sensations. It all seemed to spin out of control. When the deep growl of pleasure clawed its way out of his throat and reverberated against her clit, her last vestige of conscious control exploded in an incendiary flash. The most intense climax of her life crashed through her body. Wave after wave of orgasmic euphoria claimed her.

Then she felt Dane shudder. He pulled his cock out of her mouth a moment before his climax released spurts of semen.

"I didn't want to presume..." His barely discernible words were a husky whisper.

She responded to his concern by placing a tender kiss on his cock head and flicking the remaining droplets into her mouth with her tongue while gently cradling his balls.

Neither of them moved as the exhaustion swept over their bodies. Only the vibrations of the butt plug continued to accompany their combined gasps for air.

****

Sunlight filtered in around the edges of the bedroom drapes. Dane opened one eye and tried to focus on the clock across the room. Eleven o'clock. It had been about six hours since they fell asleep. He glanced at the nightstand. Three empty condom packets, and then there were the numerous adventures that hadn't required a condom.

And the best part was, Shasta Brooks still nestled next to him as she slept. He watched her, the rise and fall of her perfect breasts as she took slow even breaths. Hot sex. Sizzling passion. Tender intimacy. And a closeness he couldn't even begin to describe. One he hadn't believed possible.

As much as he wanted to be with her, the possibility of where their time together could lead equally frightened him. Perhaps even more than he was willing to admit. Being committed to someone, not being able to do as he pleased when he pleased, needing to take someone else into consideration when a decision had to be made…all of it scared him. He had sworn he would never be tied to anyone, especially after what he had experienced in the past.

And then there was the deeper fear, the one that said he didn't know how to take care of or participate in a committed relationship. He had no role models during his upbringing, no one to learn from. If he tried and failed, where would that leave him? The concept of losing Shasta…well, it was unfathomable.

Shasta stirred, intruding into his thoughts and providing him with a welcome distraction from the direction those thoughts had been headed.

"Good morning, lovely lady. How did you sleep?" He pulled her to him and placed a soft kiss on her lips.

"Mmm…I slept marvelously well." She kept her eyes shut as she ran her hands across the hard planes of his chest. "My sleep was filled with erotic dreams that didn't even come close to the reality of last night."

He kissed her again, a kiss that started out gentle but quickly escalated as she returned his ardor. He ran his hand down her back and across her perfectly rounded rear end, then slipped his fingers between her legs, seeking out the moist heat of her pussy. Her soft moan fed into his rapidly growing arousal. His rigid shaft pulsed with desire. "How about breakfast in bed?"

He teased the corner of her mouth with his lips, moved down the side of her neck and finally arrived at her breasts. He suckled for a moment, then allowed her nipple to slip from his mouth. "I've found something to nibble on, and I can't think of a better way to start the day."

She wiggled her hand between their bodies until she could wrap it around his cock. "Mmm…I found something I'd like to get closer to." His soft moan in response to her touch excited her as much as the feel of his hardness.

Tremors of increased arousal coursed through her body as he worked his fingers in and out of her pussy. Her quick pelvic thrust set her hips in a rocking motion against his hand. All the intensity of the night's lovemaking came rushing back, engulfing her in the heated frenzy. Once again, he had propelled her to the ultimate pinnacle of pleasure.

He had manipulated her clit in a manner that had produced multiple orgasms for her last night, and this morning was no different. The deliciously familiar sensations pulsed deep inside. Her abdominal walls clenched and her clit throbbed. Her entire body teetered on the brink of release. Cries of rapture accompanied the convulsions as her pussy muscles squeezed his fingers. Her chest heaved as she filled her lungs with air.

Shasta grabbed one of the remaining condom packets from the nightstand and ripped it open with trembling fingers as she scooted back until she straddled his thighs. Slowly, sensually, almost as if it was an integral part of a mating ritual, she rolled the condom onto his rigid shaft. The glow of passion reached out to her from the depths of his turquoise eyes.

Dane grabbed her around the waist, lifted, then gradually lowered her wet pussy onto his stiff erection. Inch by inch until she was completely impaled on his hard shaft. Her pussy muscles seized him and held on. He paused to catch his breath, the power of the sensation literally robbing him of the ability to breathe.

Her uncombed auburn hair framed her face in a wild display of sensual earthiness, a look that radiated pure sex. Her emerald eyes held the same wildly uninhibited look that always jumped his heartbeat into high gear. And after last night, he knew just how delightfully and surprisingly uninhibited she could be.

He managed to force out a few words. "You are the sexiest...hottest...most exciting woman..."

She rocked back and forth, each motion tugging his

cock and spurring his arousal. He cupped her swaying breasts, kneading the firm flesh. Her movements became more erratic, her rocking more of a grinding as the levels of euphoria drove her harder and faster. The look of total abandon covered her face with a smoldering desire that reached out to him, sending a hot jolt through his body directly to his throbbing cock.

He grabbed her hips to guide her into a rhythmic ride. Her level of arousal excited him. Seeing her in the throes of orgasm, feeling her pussy walls contract sharply around his shaft, experiencing her convulsions as they surged through her body…everything about her pushed him closer and closer to his own release.

She gave a final gasp and slumped forward against his chest, triggering the churning in his balls, followed by hard spasms shuddering through his body as his semen gushed into the condom.

She trembled in his arms, her gasps for air matching his own. He caressed her shoulders, skimmed his hands down her back and cupped her ass. He held her hips tightly against his. He didn't want to let go, to relinquish his hold on the precious gift she had shared with him…the gift of herself. A gift to treasure for all time.

After several minutes of quiet, he placed tender kisses on her forehead, her cheek and her lips. She responded with the same. He savored the taste of her mouth and reveled in the creamy texture of her skin.

She lifted her head from his shoulder, then raised up so that she sat straddling his hips. She brushed a stray lock of his tawny blond hair from his forehead. "Now that's the way to start the morning. I'll race you to the shower, then we'll see what's in my refrigerator for breakfast." She glanced at the clock. "Maybe we'd better think about lunch instead."

****

"I'm back." Dane's voice called from the front door.

"On the patio. Grab yourself a cup of coffee and join me." Shasta listened as he went to the bedroom, then to the kitchen. She heard the refrigerator door open, then close. A warm sensation flowed through her. It felt very comfortable having him walk into her house and make himself at home. What would it be like to have him call to her from the front door every evening to announce that he was home?

A moment later, he appeared at the patio door, carrying a mug of coffee, and settled himself into the chair next to hers.

A sly grin played across his lips, almost like a little boy with a secret he couldn't hold in one minute longer. "I stopped by the grocery store and picked up a little something for later."

"Oh? Anything you'd care to tell me about?"

He leaned over and brushed a soft kiss across her lips. "It's a surprise."

"You weren't gone very long. You must not live far from me."

"All this time, I've only lived about ten minutes away from you and never knew it. I only had to grab a few things from home. It's not like I was packing for a long trip, just the weekend."

His words circulated through her mind. *Just the weekend.* Was that all it was to him, just a fantasy weekend of fun and games? Monday morning things return to the way they were?

She watched him as he sipped his coffee. His gaze seemed to be fixed on something far away, something not even real, as he stared out across her backyard. What thoughts went through his mind? What did he want? A moment of sadness welled inside her. She looked away.

What secrets had he held on to when he started to explain his night job as the Macho Marauder, male stripper extraordinaire?

He placed his hand on top of hers and gave it an intimate little squeeze as he offered a warm smile. "It's a beautiful day. Would you like to do something? Take a ferry boat ride? Do a harbor tour? Go for a walk along the waterfront?"

She returned his smile. "Any of those would be fun."

"Let's do a harbor tour, then have dinner somewhere. How about the restaurant at the top of the Space Needle? I'll call and make dinner reservations."

"You mean like an actual date?" She may have injected a teasing quality into her voice accompanied by a wry grin, but the question had a much deeper meaning to her, something not nearly as casual as she had made it sound.

He held eye contact for a long moment, as if trying to delve to the bottom of her soul in a quest to know everything about her. A little tremor of anxiety fluttered inside her. Incredible hot sex. A no holds barred fantasy weekend. She could keep up that charade, not wanting to put any undue pressure on him.

But for her? Things had moved fast and furious, leaving the original fantasy far behind and presenting her with a new one. A fantasy that she didn't dare dwell on or mention.

A fantasy about Dane Wingate and what the future could be with him.

"Yes." He pulled her into his arms. His voice dropped to a mere whisper as he cradled her head against his shoulder. "The date I should have asked you for a long time ago."

As much as his words touched her heart with an intimate warmth, they probably meant far more to her than he intended. She had to keep things in the proper perspective.

****

The afternoon passed quickly, a time of relaxed togetherness. They strolled along the waterfront hand in hand, took the Elliott Bay boat tour of the harbor, then drove to the Seattle Center for an early dinner at the Space Needle. They were seated at a window table in the revolving restaurant and enjoyed the marvelous changing views of Puget Sound, the Cascade Mountains and the Olympic Mountains as they ate. To all outward appearances, they seemed to be a couple in love.

As they returned to Shasta's house, the emotions fueled by a perfect day with the most incredible man she had ever known welled inside her only to be tempered by the same nagging concern that had been gnawing at her. The one that said he was hiding something, and that something represented the wedge preventing them from truly being together.

"I can't remember the last time I spent such a delightful afternoon. It's been a long time since I was at the Space Needle." Her feelings for him choked her words. "Thank you for dinner."

"Thank you for sharing it with me." Dane took her

hand in his and brushed a tender kiss across her lips. His voice turned soft as he fought to keep the emotion out of it, an emotion he wasn't ready to confide or share. An emotion that didn't...that *couldn't*...have any place in his life. At least not at that time. "It's been a long time since I've taken an afternoon to be carefree and enjoy myself. And to have an entire weekend to spend with someone so special."

He knew he needed to change the subject before he said more than he wanted to and ended up revealing too much about his past. Last night had been incredible, and today had been a perfect day, starting when he woke up with Shasta sleeping next to him. He didn't want to ruin the rest of the weekend by bringing unpleasant realities into it. Especially the reality that said he had gotten in over his head where Shasta Brooks was concerned. He feared he might be falling in love with her, and he couldn't allow it to happen.

"There's still a couple of bottles of champagne left from your birthday party. Let's enjoy a glass on the patio." He tilted his head to one side and winked at her. "And then, as soon as it's dark, maybe we can take advantage of the hot tub again. And while we're at it take advantage of each other, too."

She smiled. "I'll get the glasses. You open the champagne."

They sat on the patio, sipping champagne and enjoying the last ribbons of color streaking across the night sky. Shasta couldn't stop her mind from wandering to thoughts she didn't want to deal with. It wasn't anything real, only a feeling that said he had started to distance himself. Not physically but personally. And she didn't understand why. Did she dare mention it? Pry into his private life? In some ways, he was so open and forth right, but there still remained the secrets he guarded.

Granted, they had most certainly shared incredible sex that put their relationship on a much deeper level than two people just starting to date. But it had been physical. He had fucked her into mind boggling orgasms more intense than any she had ever experienced, but there was an emotional intimacy that seemed to hover on the sidelines without being truly a part of their time together. It left her uncertain about what to say or how much she could expect.

With the patio cloaked in darkness, Dane removed the cover from the hot tub. He took Shasta's hand. "Do you still want to enjoy the hot tub for a while?"

His touch warmed her, a combination of sensual heat and tenderness. "Yes. The hot tub sounds marvelous."

They went to her bedroom and quickly discarded their clothes. Once again, she marveled at the hard planes of his chest, his broad shoulders, athletic build and a truly beautiful cock that made her pussy wet just looking at it. And the knowledge of how it felt inside her—of the way it filled her tunnel with deep sure strokes, the pulsing heat that radiated from it—set her heart pounding and her blood racing hot through her veins.

If they made love ten times a day every day for the rest of her life, she still would want more of him. The fact that she was in lust with him was not in doubt, but heaven help her, she was on the fast track to love.

He pulled her into his embrace, ran his fingers through the silky strands of her hair, then held her close. He couldn't get enough of the feel of her bare skin, her taste, the way her pussy tugged at his cock, the indescribable beauty and glow on her face as the orgasmic convulsions claimed her.

But he had gone past mere lust the first time he kissed her. He was closing in on love and couldn't allow it. He released her from his embrace, all except her hand. They paused at the door to the patio, turned out the lights, pulled the drapes open and stepped outside. They settled into the water, Dane seated on the bench with Shasta straddling his legs and facing him as she had before.

He pulled her close, his breath ragged as he sought out her breasts. He teased her nipple with the tip of his tongue, then drew it into his mouth. He suckled gently at first, but it quickly became more fervent as his ardor increased. How could he continue to deny the emotional need that coursed through him, feelings as hot and fast as his physical need to have his cock buried deep inside her pussy?

He felt as if his life was being torn apart—what he wanted on one hand and on the other what he knew he needed to do. And the longer he stayed with her, the more difficult it would be to leave.

At that moment the world he had been able to glimpse, the possibility of what the future could be, crashed around him. Did he have the right to make love to her again, knowing he had no choice but to leave? To take one last memory of the most joyous and happiest time of his life?

It had only been twenty-four hours since the shock of realizing that she was the birthday girl, but it had been a very full twenty-four hours. Perhaps it was selfish of him, but he needed to have that last remnant to cling to.

He lifted her off of him, grabbed a couple of towels, then led her inside the house. Neither of them spoke as they walked to her bedroom. Somehow he had to figure out a way to make everything all right. But how?

He pulled her into bed, wrapped her in his arms and held her. Just held her and nothing more for what seemed like a long time. He didn't want to let go but knew he couldn't stay, at least not for much longer. He didn't have the right to expect anyone to put up with his lifestyle, not at this time. Not until he could call his life his own again.

Dane shifted his weight, which made his arousal more obvious as his erection pressed against Shasta's stomach. Her pussy tingled. Her heart beat faster. To fall asleep every night in his arms after making love, to wake up each morning in his arms and start the day by making love...the concept settled over her like a warm embrace.

A moment of caution told her not to get too comfortable with that idea. Eventually Monday morning would arrive. Dane would go home, and she would go back to work. The girls would ask, and she would confide to them with a sly grin that she tried out some of her new birthday toys without mentioning the most precious and incredible birthday gift of all.

Without warning, his mouth captured hers, and all concerns evaporated in a surge of hot passion. His tongue meshed with hers in a mating ritual that promised more of the pleasure he had provided in the last twenty-four hours. Yet it conveyed a much more emotion-laden type of passion—hot desire tempered by a much deeper connection of caring and devotion.

Shasta totally melted into his tender care, and at that moment, he became the center of her universe. He gently suckled at her breast, his mouth both inflaming her senses and calming her worries. She ran her fingers through his thick tawny hair and caressed his broad shoulders. His erection throbbed against her thigh, creating a pulsing response deep inside her. She heard the soft moan, but it took a moment for her to realize it had come from her rather than him.

He inserted his finger between her pussy lips, invading the moist heat. She let out a quick gasp and arched her hips against his hand, letting him know she wanted more. Heat spiraled inside her, elevating her arousal to a level just below the ultimate. She cried out when he stimulated her clit, her body convulsing in delicious orgasm.

He grabbed the condom packet and ripped it open.

A moment later, his cock filled her pussy as no one else ever had, ever could. With her legs wrapped around his hips, she met each of his down strokes with an upward thrust. His mouth again captured hers in a kiss that both demanded and promised the pleasure hovering on the horizon. They moved in harmony, the sensations again building to a crescendo peak.

She loved him. She no longer had any doubts. In twenty-four hours, it had gone from fantasizing, to lust and finally to love. She permitted the thought to enter her mind and linger there without any attempt to censor it.

His shaft moved smoothly in and out of her, each stroke reaching to the depths of her wet channel, delving deep. Her ragged breathing matched his labored breaths. His strokes shortened, becoming quicker and harder. They rushed toward the final moment of release, exploding in an intense climax of shared ecstasy.

Yes, she truly loved him.

Dane held her tightly as the spasms claimed his body. He would never be able to make love to another woman, never know the total rapture Shasta provided him. It was a bittersweet moment. He wanted to be with her always, but he knew he couldn't.

He also knew that the longer he stayed in her bed, the more difficult it would be to do what had to be done. He could not stay another night. Could not wake up one more morning with her in his arms, knowing that he could not ask her to share his very unsettled and complicated life.

Not now. Not yet. Maybe not ever.

He twined his fingers through the silky strands of her hair and cradled her head to his shoulder. He couldn't put it off any longer. He kissed her once more, then slipped out of bed and went to the bathroom, taking his overnight bag with him.

Shasta sat upright in bed, shocked out of her blissful contentment when Dane stepped from the bathroom fully dressed. A myriad of confused thoughts swirled through her mind, none of them forming into a cohesive thought. A cold shiver of fear told her what her mind refused to accept.

She tried to read the expression that covered his handsome features but couldn't discern anything definite. But his eyes told another story, one of deep pain and nearly unbearable despair. Her mouth went dry. Her throat tried to close off. She managed to croak out a single word. "Dane?"

He reached out toward her but let his hand drop before making physical contact. "I'm so sorry, Shasta. I can't…"

Chapter Four

Shasta balanced her cash drawer and prepared to leave work. A week had passed since the night Dane left her, each day more devastating than the one before.

Friday had finally come to a close, and she drove straight home as she had done each evening, hoping against hope that she would hear from Dane. She had tried to understand, tried to put herself in his position as he told her about his life being too unsettled to be able to form any attachments. That he couldn't expect her to put up with the life of a male stripper. She had even gone so far as to assure him she understood.

But she didn't. She had cried herself to sleep Saturday night after he left, then spent all day Sunday hoping he would have a change of heart and return to her house. By Sunday night she had to accept the truth. It was a marvelous fantasy, the most incredible twenty-four hours of her life, but it had ended in pain and bittersweet disappointment. It was with a heavy heart that she went to work Monday morning, knowing she would have to face her friends and their comments about the Macho Marauder performing at her birthday party while hiding her agony behind a façade.

After changing from her work clothes into comfortable jeans and a T-shirt, she went to her refrigerator to retrieve the bottle of champagne left over from her birthday. She paused as she reached for the bottle, then grabbed the can of whipped cream instead. When he had gone home Saturday morning to get some clean clothes and returned with the topping to go with the chocolate body paint, he must have surely intended to spend the weekend…a fantasy weekend filled with even more treats than they had already indulged.

Why had he changed his mind? What had happened to turn everything upside down? She had asked herself that question a hundred times but had not discovered an answer that made any sense.

She replaced the can of whipped cream, picked up the champagne bottle, opened it and poured herself a glass. At least work kept her busy during the day, but the nights had been so horribly lonely. They seemed to close in around her. And now the weekend. She sank into the softness of her favorite chair, took a sip of her champagne, then set the glass on the end table and closed her eyes.

Dane's handsome face immediately appeared on the screen of her mind. Every torrid moment of hot sex assaulted her senses, making her pussy tingle with excitement and throb with need. Each tender moment and gentle caress touched her heart in a way nothing else ever had.

And with each passing day, her heart had broken a little more.

Her eyelids felt heavy. An emotional exhaustion washed over her as she slowly drifted into an uneasy sleep.

It seemed like only seconds later when a knocking on her front door forced her eyes open. The room was dark. She turned on the table lamp and glanced at her watch. Nearly midnight. The insistent knocking turned into a determined pounding. She pushed herself out of the chair and made her way across the room.

She opened the door and stared in disbelief, not fully comprehending what she saw. Was she still asleep and having a dream? Was her imagination playing tricks on her? She tried to swallow the anxiety welling inside her as she reached out toward him. Was he real? A flesh and blood man standing on her porch? Her hand touched the hard planes of his chest. The strong beat of his heart resonated to her fingertips.

"Dane?"

The uncertainty covered his face and filled his voice. "May I come in?"

"Uh…" She shook her head to try and clear the fuzziness. "Of course." She stepped aside and closed the door behind him. After taking a calming breath to steady her shattered nerves, she turned to face him. "This is a surprise. What are you doing here and so late at night?"

"I just finished my last performance of the night at the club."

He started to reach for her but withdrew his hand. "I tried to stay away. I kept telling myself you were better off not having to deal with my problems and my currently fucked up life. You deserve better than what I can offer at this time. You deserve a man who can be with you, not one who spends most nights at some piece of shit club having strange women try to pull his clothes off and grab his cock. There is no way I can expect any woman to stand idly by and simply accept the life of a male stripper." He stared at the floor as if not quite knowing what else to say.

Shasta blinked several times in an attempt to hold

back her tears. She didn't know what to say or how to respond either. With cautious optimism, she allowed a glimmer of hope to seep in. Her voice was anything but confident as she tried to inject as much control as she could. "Then why are you here?"

"I...I don't know. I'm not sure." He ran his hand across the back of his neck and shook his head as if trying to clear the confusion.

Then he looked up and made eye contact with her. She had absolutely no control over her mind or body. She couldn't focus her thoughts or slow her racing pulse. Her breath caught in her lungs. The mesmerizing pull of his presence had her trapped in the spell that had been cast over her the second she saw him standing on her porch. She couldn't hold back her tears as they spilled over and slowly trickled down her cheeks.

The pain in her eyes was more than Dane could handle, more than anything he had ever encountered. It clawed at his heart, ripping apart what was left of it. He couldn't stop himself from wrapping his arms around her and pulling her to him. It felt so good to be able to hold her again. He cradled her head against his shoulder and placed a tender kiss on her forehead.

"I'm so sorry, Shasta. I never meant to hurt you. I...I mean..." He held her tighter. He didn't want to ever let go of her. Never again.

He swallowed down the trepidation trying to push its way into his reality. He had to make a choice...overcome the fear of even attempting a committed relationship or else risk losing the person who meant more to him than anyone in the world. His heart pounded so loudly, surely she must be able to hear it. He closed his eyes for a moment as he gathered his courage.

"I don't want to lose you." Once the words were out of his mouth, it was as if the flood gates had been opened wide. "I was an only child. My mother and father argued constantly. I grew up in the middle of shouting matches, bitter words and accusations. When I was fifteen, my father walked out the door and never came back." He tried to force a calm to the chaos knotting in his stomach, but it didn't work.

"My mother sank deeper into her bitterness and spent all her time complaining. I felt like I was drowning in all the negative energy. I wanted nothing more out of life than to get as far away as I could from anything having to do with my childhood and teen years." He nuzzled his cheek against her head as he collected his thoughts.

"Several years later, when my mother became ill, I had no choice but to return and take care of her and then make good on her medical expenses. But it was the last straw. I wanted nothing to do with family ever again. When your only role models in life are a father who deserts is wife and son and a mother so filled with bitter resentment that she can only function by complaining to the point where she drives everyone away from her…well, you don't exactly feel the need or desire to embrace the concept of relationship."

He took a steadying breath before continuing. "I've just spent the most miserable week of my life. Nothing in my past was as bad as what I've been through since I walked out of here last Saturday night." He placed another kiss on her forehead as he threaded his fingers through her hair. "I can't imagine my life without you."

Shasta's emotions soared to the heights. His words

touched the very core of her soul. "Oh, Dane...you have no idea what it means to me to hear you say that. When you left, when I saw you walk out the door, I thought I'd die. I didn't think I'd ever see you again. This last week has been horrible. I kept telling myself no one can base a relationship on twenty-four hours of hot sex no matter how good it was. But for me it was so much more than just fun and games."

"I can't deny the truth any longer. I love you, Shasta. You mean everything to me." He caressed her shoulders, holding her tightly. "This has all happened so quickly, maybe even too quickly. But I've never had anything feel so right."

"I love you, too, Dane. You're right. It all happened so fast, but I know it's true. I know it in my heart."

"I quit the club tonight. The Macho Marauder has made his last appearance. I'll find some other way of paying off the rest of the expenses. It will take me longer, but it will be worth it, knowing we can be together."

She circled her arms around his neck and brushed a soft kiss across his lips. "Maybe I can help you with that. I live very simply and have been able to save quite a bit. How much do you still owe?"

"I don't want your money. I'll figure out another way of handling it."

"But I want to help."

A wicked grin tugged at the corners of his mouth. "Money isn't the pressing matter right now." He took her hand and rubbed it against the prominent bulge at his crotch.

She returned his grin with a knowing one of her

own. "Yes, I see what you mean. I'm sure I can help you with that…if you'll let me."

He wrapped his arms around her again. His smile faded, seriousness emanating from the depths of his eyes. "I love you so much, Shasta." The heartfelt words tickled across her ear. "I don't know exactly how the future is going to unfold, but as long as we're together, that's all I can ask for, that's everything I want."

"That's what I want, too."

He captured her mouth with a loving kiss, one filled with the emotion coursing through his body. He didn't hold anything back, allowing his deep and abiding love for her to finally come through. And she returned that love as their souls merged into one.

It was Shasta who broke the kiss. "I'll join you in the bedroom in a minute."

He looked at her questioningly, obviously not knowing exactly what to make of her words. "Okay." He headed down the hallway.

She watched his retreating form, then turned toward the kitchen. She grabbed the can of whipped cream from the refrigerator and hurried to catch up with him. A sexy smile lit his face when he saw what she had in her hand.

"And where, my sexy beauty, have you hidden the chocolate body paint?"

She ran her free hand across the denim covering his ass, then wiggled it into the waist band of his jeans. "Get yourself out of those clothes, and I'll show you."

He pulled his shirt over his head and let it drop to the floor, then quickly doffed the rest of his clothes. Without a moment's hesitation, she stripped off her clothes and handed him the can of whipped cream before stretching out in the middle of the bed.

Raising her arms, she beckoned him to her. His cock jumped and twitched when she spread her legs and ran the tip of her tongue over her upper lip. The glow in the depth of his eyes told her he liked what he saw, and his cock standing tall and hard told her he was ready.

He shook the whipped cream can, then took off the cap. "Looks like I arrived just in time for dessert."

Masked Encounter

Chapter One

As much as she tried, she didn't seem to have any control over her own body. Moisture seeped from between the delicate folds of her femininity. Her heart pounded in her chest and her pulse raced. Nipples puckered into taut peaks. Breasts rose and fell with each ragged breath she sucked into her lungs.

She watched, fascinated by the way he slowly peeled off his shirt, almost as if he had chosen to perform a slow strip tease for the enjoyment of an audience of one. The candle light shimmered off the hard planes of his well-defined chest. His sexy smile spoke to her, telling of all the delights the night would bring. Making eye contact with him, she held it just long enough to see the heated desire smoldering in the depths of his green eyes.

Her body trembled in anticipation of what she knew would be the hottest sex she had ever experienced. The tip of her tongue ran across her upper lip as her gaze dropped to his crotch and the noticeable bulge that promised passion beyond her wildest expectations. She scrutinized his every move as he lowered his zipper—

"Hey, Trish."

Julie's voice abruptly intruded into the fantasy, jerking Trish Andrews back into the here and now. She tried to clear the sexy image from her mind, an easier task than stopping the sensual excitement that flooded her body and dampened her panties.

"I don't know where your mind was, but you'd better get it back on work. Mr. Rutledge just pulled into the parking lot."

"What?" Her eyes widened in shock as Julie's words caught her totally off guard. "Oh, no! I didn't think he'd be in this morning." She did a quick perusal of her office, her attention drawn to the unopened mail and the fact that she hadn't even turned on her computer yet. "He just got back from London late last night. I didn't expect to see him until after lunch." She shook her head in disbelief. "The man is too much of a workaholic. He couldn't even take the morning off."

Pushing back from her desk, she extended a grateful smile toward her friend. "Thanks for the warning, Julie."

Trish had been Jonathon Rutledge's administrative assistant for the last three years and the executive vice president's secretary prior to that. When her predecessor retired, she had applied for the opening in Jonathon's office. She had worked for Rutledge Industries a total of nine years, starting right after she graduated from college. She enjoyed her job and admired the man who headed the corporation. But business acumen wasn't the only thing she admired about the dynamic, handsome and very sexy Jonathon Rutledge.

After flipping on her computer, she scurried around the office making sure everything was in its place. Now wasn't the time for her to dwell on his many attractive qualities, not the least of which was a magnetic sex appeal that had been driving her crazy for three years.

She quickly opened the mail and sorted it into stacks according to the envelope contents. She breathed a sigh of relief and poured a cup of coffee just as Jonathon Rutledge swept into her office.

She handed him the steaming mug and presented a businesslike smile. Her words were crisp and precise. "Good morning, Mr. Rutledge."

He took the coffee from her as he flashed an appreciative grin. "Ah…just what I need. I'm still functioning on London time. Thank you, Miss Andrews."

She followed him into his office. He removed his suit jacket and handed it to her. A hint of his aftershave clung to the fabric. Carrying the jacket to the closet, she took the opportunity to inhale the fragrance before hanging it up. Her fingers lingered a moment on the expensive material. Everything about Jonathon Rutledge excited her senses and fed her fantasies.

She handed him his mail. "I'm surprised to see you here."

He cocked his head and looked at her questioningly, a teasing smile tugging at the corners of his mouth. "Why? This is still my office, isn't it?"

"I meant with you having arrived from London so late last night." A hint of embarrassment tinged her words. "I had assumed you would take the morning off."

He settled in behind his large oak desk. "It was certainly tempting, but I have to put the finishing touches on the London deal."

"You have an appointment at three this afternoon with your attorney. Do you want me to reschedule it for Monday?"

"No, that won't be necessary." Jonathon loosened his tie and undid the top button of his silk shirt. He didn't like wearing a suit and tie to the office. He was far more comfortable in jeans but had acquiesced to the necessity because of his meeting at his attorney's office with the president and vice president of Premier Associates along with their attorney.

He had been trying to buy Premier Associates for over a year. It was the only reason he had returned from London on Thursday night rather than staying through the weekend.

That, and the costume party Marty Collins was hosting on Saturday night. It had been a long time since he had taken a break from his work schedule and done something just for fun. And Marty always threw fun parties.

Jonathon leaned back in his chair and watched Trish as she returned to her office. She was dressed in her normal sensible skirt and blazer, her blonde hair pulled neatly back into a bun. He had never seen her hair in any other style. Very tailored, very businesslike, very efficient.

His relationship with his employees had always been strictly business. It made for a more professional working atmosphere and prevented any personal problems that might arise from social interaction with the people who worked for him. He found it too difficult to be friends and socialize on Friday night and then be the boss again on Monday morning.

He took a swallow from his coffee mug as he allowed his thoughts to wander. Trish Andrews had been his administrative assistant for three years, but he didn't really know that much about her. He knew the surface things, but nothing truly personal. What kind of music did she listen to? What kind of movies did she go see? What kind of books did she read? Somewhere under that practical exterior there had to be a real woman. Did she ever let her hair down and have fun, or did it stay in that bun even when she wasn't at work? Was she dating anyone special? Did she go to wild parties? Drink champagne from crystal flutes? Dance until dawn?

Or better yet, did she ever lose that cool, controlled efficiency and have wild sex with a stranger? His cock twitched, followed by the unmistakable signs of arousal telling him what he already knew—he desperately needed to get laid. It had been much too long since the last time he buried his hard cock inside a desirable woman and fucked the night away.

He sucked in a calming breath and slowly exhaled as he shook his head. Even the prim and proper Miss Andrews was starting to look good to him. He took another swallow of coffee. He had too much work to do to waste time fantasizing about someone who wouldn't be his type even if she didn't work for him.

****

The low cut floor length evening gown clung to her curves, seeming more like something that had been painted on her body rather than a piece of clothing. It left just enough to the imagination to whet Jonathon Rutledge's appetite for more.

The back dipped dangerously low. The side slit reached half way up her thigh. The front seemed to be nothing more than two strips of fabric extending upward from her waist and meeting at the back of her neck while managing to barely cover and contain her breasts. There was no way she could possibly have anything on underneath.

Jonathon had noticed the stunning blonde in the red dress the moment he arrived at the party. He could almost feel the silky strands of her shoulder length hair as it tangled around his fingers. Her Mardi Gras style mask covered most of her face in feathers, sequins and glitter. Her hips swayed in a seductive glide as she walked across the floor.

He spotted his host standing at the bar and sauntered toward him, trying to appear much more casual than he felt. He kept a watchful eye on the stunning vision in the red dress as he crossed the room.

"Jonathon." Marty Collins stuck out his hand in greeting. "Good to see you. I wasn't sure you were going to make it."

"I wasn't sure, either." He shoved his mask up on his forehead, then shook hands with Marty. "I had to fly to London to salvage a business deal that was about to fall apart. I just got back night before last. I didn't want to miss the festivities." He scanned the room, noting everything that came across his line of sight. "This is quite a shindig you've thrown. It's been a long time since I attended a costume party."

"I had a lot of social obligations I owed to various business associates, so I decided to take care of all of them at once by renting the hotel ballroom and throwing a lavish masked ball."

Marty scrutinized Jonathon's costume from the buccaneer hat and head wrap bandana with attached beaded braids, the long-sleeved shirt with wide collar topped by the leather vest, the cutlass hanging from the leather belt, on down to the black boots. "Captain Jack

Sparrow, I presume?" An amused grin spread across his face. "Aren't you a little off course? We're nowhere near the Caribbean."

"This was my second choice." A sly grin tugged at the corners of his mouth. "I had planned to wear just the mask and a pair of black socks while sporting an impressive erection and claim I was dressed as a porn star."

Jonathon glanced toward the French doors leading to the large balcony. The rain continued to pound against the glass without any sign of let up. "Unfortunately the weather turned cold. I decided a black mask and black socks with only a cock cozy to keep me warm wouldn't have been appropriate even if the cock cozy looked like a hot dog bun."

Marty's appreciative laugh filled the air. "Well, if anyone could get away with something like that, it would be you."

Jonathon grabbed a glass of champagne from the tray as the waiter passed by. "Of course," he indicated the stunning blonde vision across the room, "that's a body that would have kept the blood rushing hot and my soldier standing at full attention no matter how cold the weather was." A twitch in his groin told him just how accurate that statement had been. He took a swallow from his glass as he watched the object of his fascination for a moment.

"So, tell me, Marty…who is she and why haven't I ever seen her before? One doesn't forget a body like that. Have you been keeping her all for yourself?" Jonathon gave his friend a teasing wink. "Does your wife know about her?"

A slight frown crossed Marty's face. "I have no

idea who she is. I had assumed she was someone's date, but she doesn't seem to be with anyone in particular. She's danced with several people but never the same man twice. She appears to be here solo."

Jonathon pulled himself up to his full six foot-two inch height, squared his broad shoulders and pulled his mask back into place. "Don't concern yourself with this problem. I'll get to the bottom of this or my name isn't Captain Jack Sparrow." *The bottom, the top, the front, the back, that most desirable place nestled between those incredible legs...*

He placed his empty champagne glass on a tray, grabbed two full glasses and carried them across the room.

"Allow me to introduce myself. Captain Jack Sparrow at your service." He handed her one of the glasses of champagne, gave a courtly bow, and took her hand in his. Rather than kissing the back of her hand, he kissed the inside of her wrist. The heat of her blood rushing through her veins warmed his lips. "May I ask what such a demure, innocent maiden is doing here all by herself?"

Her gaze slowly traveled from the top of his hat down to his boots, then back to his face. He could see the sparkle in her blue eyes and her delicious looking mouth, but the rest of her face remained hidden behind her mask.

There was something vaguely familiar about her eyes and mouth, but he couldn't place where he'd seen them or who they belonged to. Or even whether it was real or just his imagination. An image popped into his mind, a picture of his rigid cock sliding in and out of that delicious looking mouth with her perfect lips forming a seal around his shaft.

She ran the tip of her tongue across her upper lip. "Tell me, Captain Sparrow," she dropped her voice to a seductive whisper, "what makes you think I'm so innocent?"

His breath caught in his lungs. A tightness pulled across his chest. An incendiary wave of pure lust swept through his body and settled in his groin. If she was trying to entice him, she was wasting her time. He was already aroused, his burgeoning erection starting to strain against the front of his trousers.

He flashed his most charming smile. "That sounds like an interesting topic of conversation." He wasn't pleased with the slight huskiness that clung to his words, something he believed showed a lack of control on his part. "Would you like to go someplace quiet so we can discuss it? Thoroughly delve into every facet of innocence versus reality?"

She returned his smile. "It would be my pleasure."

"I hope so because I know it's going to be mine." He placed his hand at the small of her back, his fingers coming in contact with bare skin. His arousal stiffened, well on its way to being a full hard erection. It took all his will power to keep from moving his hand lower and skimming it inside her dress until he could cup the round globes of her ass. He pressed gently against her back to direct her toward the door.

They walked down the hall to the elevators. Just being near her kept his cock standing up and demanding attention. His nostrils flared as the intoxicating scent of her perfume wafted across his senses. It prompted visions of hot, wanton sex. It promised a night he instinctively knew he would never forget.

The elevator doors opened and three people got off. He stood aside and indicated she should enter the car.

"Where are we going?" Trish trailed her hand across the front of Jonathon's shirt as she stepped inside the elevator car. The sensation of the silk against her fingertips was almost as exciting as the hard planes of his chest beneath the fabric. Almost as exciting as the moment his hand had touched her bare back.

Her pulse jumped and her breathing quickened. Dampness seeped across her mound and heat spread to her thighs. The soft fabric of her dress caressed her breasts. Her nipples puckered into taut points of need. She knew his hands would soon be doing the caressing, then his mouth, and the knowledge pulsed hot and deep inside her body.

He reached past her shoulder and pushed the button for the twentieth floor. As soon as the doors closed, the elevator started its ascent. The swiftness of his movements took her by surprise as he backed her into the corner. His mouth hovered just above hers, his hands planted against the elevator wall on each side of her head. So temptingly close she could almost taste him. The tantalizing whiff of his sexy aftershave wasn't enough to detract from the clean masculine scent that filled her lungs and raced through her veins. Her senses tingled with anticipation of what the evening would bring.

"I never party, drink and debauch innocent—" he flicked the tip of his tongue across her lip as he leaned his body against hers, "and not so innocent maidens— then try to drive home. Since the party is at a hotel, I booked a room for the night."

His nearness nearly took her breath away, making the simple task of talking increasingly difficult. "That's very astute of you, very forward thinking."

"Aye...when you're accustomed to plundering the high seas, you need to be prepared for any eventuality." The timbre of his smooth masculine voice did as much to seduce her senses as his words. With a quick pelvic thrust, he shoved his hardened sex against her. The contact gave her a quick sample of what he had to offer and sent a sharp surge of need ricocheting through her body.

"My room will be a nice quiet place where we can continue our *conversation* undisturbed."

"That sounds like the perfect place to have an intimate...uh...*conversation*."

Trish thought she knew what she was doing, had considered all the angles when she formulated her plan. But she woefully under estimated one facet. She hadn't realized just how potent his sexual magnetism could be until he pressed against her.

Tremors of arousal shuddered through her body, demanding attention. She wanted Jonathon Rutledge's obvious arousal buried deep inside her. She *needed* the feel of his hard shaft completely filling her. It was a fantasy that had dominated her dreams at night and propelled her daydreams during her waking hours for the last three years. And now it was stronger and more demanding than ever.

He removed his mask, then reached for hers. She quickly raised her hand to stop him. He looked at her quizzically. "You won't take your mask off? Then the least you can do is tell me your name."

"No. Let's play out a fantasy—two strangers

spending the night making love. No strings, no recriminations, no guilt, no worries about what the morning will bring."

"Spending the night with a sexy seductress," his husky voice whispered across her ear, "is definitely a fantasy I'll willingly indulge." He brought his mouth down on hers, capturing her very breath. It was a hungry kiss that told of long pent up needs, a kiss that demanded everything and promised as much in return.

Jonathon ground his arousal against the flat of her stomach. She slipped her arms around his neck. Her breasts pressed against his silk shirt, her tautly puckered nipples teasing his already highly aroused senses. Her ragged breathing matched his, two people caught up in the same swirl of desire.

He thrust his tongue between her lips and met an eager response as he twined it with hers in an erotic ritual of seduction. Her mouth tasted every bit as delicious as it looked, as delicious as he knew the rest of her body would be.

An all-consuming need burned inside him. If she was even half as hot as he felt, they had the potential of setting off the fire sprinklers at the very least—at the most, reducing the room to charred remains. He edged his hand inside the soft piece of fabric covering her breast. He cupped her fullness, the sensation leaving his fingers literally tingling. Her body trembled beneath his touch as he inched the material aside. A moment later he had his mouth at her breast, suckling as he teased her hardened nipple with his tongue. Her throaty moan of submission doubled the excitement racing through his body.

Somewhere in the back of his mind he became

aware of the elevator slowing to a stop. He reluctantly allowed her nipple to slip from his mouth and released her from his hold. He smoothed the front of her dress back into place.

"I think we're at my floor." His voice held a husky quality that he didn't seem to be able to control any more than he could dictate to the hard erection straining against the crotch of his pants.

A moment later the elevator doors opened. He tried to force a smoothness to his labored breathing while escorting her down the hall to his room. He had been nearly frantic to have her. He would have gladly taken her right there in the elevator if they hadn't arrived at the twentieth floor. He needed to slow things down. This wasn't a fast fuck in a darkened hallway up against a wall. They were at his room where they had all night to explore and enjoy each other in every way possible.

And that's just what he planned to do.

As soon as they were inside, he put out the *Do Not Disturb* sign and set the security lock. He didn't want any unexpected interruptions to intrude.

Then he turned toward her. She stood next to the bed, looking like a combination of perfect lady and wanton sex goddess—a fascinating and incredibly alluring blend. Her puckered nipples protruded against her dress. It was all he could do to maintain some semblance of propriety when what he really wanted to do was rip off her dress, throw her down on the bed and fuck her long and hard until they both dissolved into a puddle of spent flesh.

He tossed aside the mask, headgear, and sword belonging to his costume, then toed off his boots. She remained perfectly still as if waiting to see what he would do. Only the rise and fall of her breasts with her ragged breathing gave away her state of arousal. That and the heated glow in the depths of her eyes.

He ran his fingers along the line of her jaw, down the side of her neck and across her shoulder. The quality of her skin was unlike anything he had ever felt before, a smooth creamy texture that sent a shudder of heated anticipation rippling through his body.

Jonathon slipped the dress off her shoulders and allowed it to fall to her waist. Her firm bare breasts were capped by tautly puckered dusky pink nipples just begging for the pleasure of his mouth. He stepped in closer. She wasn't wearing a bra, but what about panties? The way the dress dipped so low in the back, lower than her waist, he wondered what she could possibly be wearing underneath. He also knew he was going to thoroughly enjoy finding out.

"Tell me, my sexy seductress. Is the bottom half of you as bare and delicious as the top half?" He traced his finger across the swell of her breasts, first one then the other, before running his fingertip between her breasts and continuing down her body until he reached her navel. She trembled beneath his touch.

"Is this dress the only thing touching your skin?" His words were part spoken and part husky rasp. "The only thing keeping me from exploring the treasure buried between your thighs?"

"No quite. But I'm sure you're about to find out for yourself." She stepped out of her high heels. "I'm sure there's lots here for both of us to discover if we apply ourselves, many things to explore before the night is over."

He heard a low groan, one that spoke of deep need

as well as desire. A groan that had clawed its way out of his own throat. A groan that betrayed the smooth exterior he tried to project. She was unlike anyone he had ever met. She was hot, delicious and very ready yet there was something hidden, something she didn't want him to see, something more than merely hiding her face behind a mask.

It also presented itself in the way she seemed to be waiting for him to take action, almost as if she didn't know what to do or how to proceed. It left him with the uncomfortable impression that she wasn't the experienced playmate she pretended to be. It was almost as if she was two people, hot sex kitten on one hand yet reserved lady on the other. He shook away the thought. It was a dilemma that would have to wait until another time.

He had been working too hard for too long without a break. If she was, indeed, two people, then tonight he wanted the one who was hot and ready. The one whose mere presence had totally seduced his senses and had his cock hard and ready practically from the moment he set eyes on her. The need had been building inside him for too long to worry about second guessing his good fortune. The side of her that seemed more demure would have to wait.

He sat on the edge of the bed and pulled her in front of him. He caught one of her nipples in his mouth and suckled as he ran his hands inside the back of her dress. It took only a moment for his fingers to reach the garter belt and discover that she wasn't wearing any panties.

The breath caught in his lungs. His fingertips tingled with a surge of excitement. His hungry mouth took in more of her breast, sucking with an increased intensity. Cupping the perfect globes of her ass cheeks, he squeezed the delectably firm flesh.

Trish's legs trembled as the sensations coursed through her body, accompanied by a hungry need pulsing between her legs. His mouth...his hands...he was everything she knew he would be, and the night was still young.

She thought she would be able to stand there and allow his tantalizing seduction to continue, to revel in the delights of his touch, but her desire to touch him was more than she could control. She snaked her fingers through his thick dark hair. His mouth may have been on her breast, but the core of her excitement was much lower. The heat spread, the moisture dampened her entire pussy.

It had been over a year since she last had sex and that had been a less than stellar experience. In fact, it had left her unfulfilled and frustrated. Stimulated but without an orgasm. In retrospect, she had only dated him because he bore a vague resemblance to Jonathon Rutledge. Since then, only her vibrator had been between her legs. It was adequate in relieving that sexual itch, but nothing more.

And now she had the real thing all to herself and one night to make all her fantasies come true.

His movements were not as smooth as she had assumed they would be as he tugged on her dress, inching it down her hips then letting it drop to the floor where it pooled at her feet. It was almost as if he had been forcing himself to take it slow.

He leaned back on his elbows. A moment of eye contact was long enough for her to see the passion shining in the depths of his green eyes. She had seen it a thousand times in her dreams and fantasies, but this time it was real.

And that glow of passion was all for her.

Her insides quivered and her heart pounded. A moment of panic invaded her reality. He was a very dynamic man. She was limited in her experience of anything beyond the basic missionary position. Would she be able to satisfy all his needs and desires? Would he find her lack of experience a turn off? She forced her negative thoughts aside. Now was not the time for doubts.

She stood in front of him. The red lace garter belt framed the blonde curls covering her sex. Red satin ribbons held up her sheer black stockings. His gaze skimmed her body, then came to rest on the feathery softness decorating her pussy. He touched her breasts again, then ran a finger lightly over her skin from the valley between her breasts down to the garter belt, then across her mound. He touched the very tip of his finger against her clit.

A sharp intake of breath followed by an earthy moan of delight escaped her throat before she could stop it. Her eyelids fluttered shut as her body trembled in response to his actions. He stroked between her legs, tracing her delicate pussy lips, then withdrew his hand and touched his wet finger to his tongue.

"I think you should leave that garter belt and your stockings on." His words came out as a husky rasp. "It's so damned sexy the way it surrounds your delicious pussy, like the perfect picture frame around an exquisite work of art."

It had taken every ounce of will power she

possessed to remain still while he skimmed his hands over her body, touched her tingling clit and ran his finger between her legs. He had been her fantasy for three years even though she knew he saw her as nothing more than an incredibly efficient employee. He normally took no more notice of her than the paint on the wall. But tonight he would be different. He would be all hers through the screaming ecstasy of multiple orgasms. She would thrill to the excitement so many other women had known in his bed. And Monday when he arrived at the office and she handed him his cup of coffee, he would never know it was her.

"You have me out of my clothes, but you're still dressed." Once again she was able to bring forth the throaty voice she had practiced in the privacy of her apartment as part of her disguise, although she couldn't control the slight quaver that surrounded her words. "I think it's time for you to get out of your clothes."

Jonathon stood up and touched the silken strands of her hair. His words were soft, his breath brushing lightly across her cheek. "I think you're right."

Chapter Two

Trish tugged Jonathon's shirt from the waist of his trousers and unfastened the top button. Then the next and the next. Her fingers trembled to the point she couldn't undo the final button. She had never undressed a man before and didn't know how to go about it. As sensual as she wanted the action to be was as awkward as she felt. She knew she was failing miserably. Was he already disappointed? Did he regret his decision to whisk her away to his hotel room?

Jonathon put his hand on top of hers and flashed a sexy grin. "Maybe you'd better let me do that." He indicated the bed. "Why don't you relax, and I'll join you in a moment?"

She returned his smile with an inviting one of her own. She leaned forward and flicked the tip of her tongue across his lower lip. She had never attempted to seduce a man before. In all her thirty years, it was the most brazen thing she had ever done, except for standing there nearly naked in front of the sexiest man alive.

She may have dressed the part of sex personified, but it was a long way from the reality of who and what she was—except for tonight. She knew there would be many more firsts for her before the night was over. One forbidden night of totally unbridled wanton passion.

One forbidden night that would have to last her a

lifetime.

She eased onto the bed, but her mind was far from relaxed. The way he had grabbed her trembling hand, telling her he'd take off his own clothes—had she made a total fool of herself? Had she managed to make it perfectly clear she was way out of her element? A player who belonged in little league rather than the major leagues with him? She had already moved far outside her realm of experience.

Another hint of panic tried to make its way to the forefront, but the tingling in her clit and her tightly drawn nipples overpowered her concerns. The look on his face said he liked what he saw as his gaze traveled across her body.

She watched as he peeled off his clothes and tossed them aside in much the same way as it had happened in her day dreams. She had visualized what his body would look like so many times, but nothing in her imagination matched this reality. His hard chest, broad shoulders, strong arms, muscled legs and a tight butt were perfection as far as she was concerned.

A rush of heat and moisture flooded between her legs. His cock stood tall and proud—the thick shaft with the clearly defined engorged veins, the head a rapidly darkening purple. She had not had the opportunity to see that many fully erect male organs in person with the lights on, but she could not imagine one more impressive than what she was staring at.

She reached for one of the pillows, arching her hips off the bed as she slipped it beneath her rear end to thrust her pussy upward so it would be more accessible. She had certainly never done that before, but had read about it. The action made her feel very sexy and uninhibited, a sensation that pleased her. The look on his face told her it delighted him, too.

"Well, my sexy seductress, that's an invitation that could make the strongest man quiver. Everything looks so good. I don't know where to begin."

That may have been what he said, but his actions made it clear that he knew exactly where he wanted to begin. He snuggled his body between her legs, spreading them as he placed his face very close to her feathered mound. She had read about oral sex and had even heard people talk about it, but she had never experienced it. She had assumed it would be part of a night of passion. Someone as sexy as Jonathon Rutledge would surely have a well-rounded repertoire, but not knowing what to expect had left her a little nervous about the prospect.

His warm breath tickled against her inner thighs sending a wave of unexpected anticipation coursing through her body. Then his lips touched her most intimate place. She drew in a hard gasp. The sensation was so much more intense than she had thought it would be. She closed her eyes as the waves of excitement assaulted her senses. She heard the moan of delight and knew it had come from her throat. She also knew she wanted much more of this new experience, this formerly forbidden treat.

He traced the outline of her pussy lips with the tip of his tongue, then flicked it against her clit. Her head jerked back against the pillow as she thrust her muff upward toward him.

Then he sucked her clit into his mouth.

Her pussy muscles spasmed in a series of rapid contractions unlike anything she had ever known as the orgasm ripped through her body. Wave after wave of pure ecstasy touched every part of her. She ran her shaky fingers through his hair, then pulled his face harder against her muff. Her hips bucked wildly, demanding more of his tantalizing lingual attentions.

"Oh, my God! That's—" The words had come out of her mouth, but she didn't recognize the breathless rasp that uttered them. "More…oh, please, more. I've never—"

Even as muddled as her mind was at the moment, she knew she had to shut up before she said something she shouldn't. Before she let him know this was all new to her. Perhaps she had already said too much. She couldn't even think. She wasn't sure exactly what she had said. All she could do was feel and experience.

Her taste exploded inside Jonathon's mouth, flowing over his tongue and filling his senses with the tantalizing spice. It was a taste he wanted to sample again and again. A taste that excited. A taste that cried out for more.

He lapped at her flowing juices, her addictive flavor filling his mouth and almost overwhelming his senses. He had never tasted a pussy as delicious or experienced such an immediate response from a woman. Her thighs tightened around his head as if she was afraid he might try to pull back. He took her clit into his mouth again, sucking on the engorged nubbin as he inhaled the aroma of her sex. His chest tightened, making it more difficult for him to breathe.

Her pussy walls grabbed at his tongue, trying to pull it deep inside. He felt her second orgasm shudder through her body and heard her whimpers and cries of fulfilled delight. It had been too long since he had been with a woman and this one was someone very special. He couldn't hold out much longer. His cock throbbed with his need for release.

He pulled his face from her steaming pussy, reluctant to give up her taste but needing his own release. Her juices matted her blonde curls against her mound, her swollen pussy lips and engorged clit, beckoning him to return. The sight, framed by the red garter belt and sheer black stockings, almost shoved him into orgasmic rapture.

He grabbed a condom packet from where he had put them on the night stand *just in case* and rolled it on. He had hoped he would get lucky, but in his wildest thought, he never thought he would end up in bed with anyone like this incredible woman.

His heart pounded in his chest as need throbbed through his body. He nudged her legs wider apart with his knee, then positioned his cock head at her opening and pushed forward. Her orgasms had made the way very wet, inviting a smooth penetration. He slowly entered her, every inch of the journey indescribable pleasure, until he was buried to the hilt.

Her walls closed around his shaft, squeezing his cock in a hot tight cocoon. The sensation nearly took away what little breath he still had. So hot. So tight. He had never experienced anything like it. He set a slow even pace, fighting to maintain control rather than surrendering to the hot passion surging through him.

His pace quickened. She was too hot, too tight and too incredible. There was no way he could hold back any longer. It had been too many months, and he was so ready. His balls pulled up tight, then his release shuddered through his body in hard spasms. His mouth found hers. He took control of it, wanting as much of her as he could take, everything she was willing to give.

He held her in his embrace, caressing her back and shoulders as he regained his composure. He couldn't remember ever being inside a woman as hot and tight as she was. Or one who tasted as sweet as she did. Or one who felt so good in his arms. One way or the other, he had to find out who she was.

She didn't have a purse of any type with her, which was a little surprising. No identification, no money, no room key, no car key, no parking claim check from the hotel's valet parking. Nothing to say who she was, how she got to the party or how she intended to get home.

He quickly disposed of the used condom. They snuggled in each other's arms for what seemed like a long time, but in reality was only about fifteen minutes. Neither spoke nor moved. It was a time of surprising closeness. A time that felt almost as emotional as it did physical.

Her unique taste continued to linger on his tongue, to fill his mouth and tease his senses. He wanted more. He also wanted to experience what he had visualized when he first encountered her…his hard shaft sliding in and out of her tempting mouth.

He acted on his fantasy by swiveling around to straddle her so that his face was at her pussy with his arms wrapped around her hips. His cock bobbed in front of her face. He immediately buried his mouth in the tasty treat. He lapped at her juices before fucking her with his tongue, each thrust dragging across her swollen clit. Her body jerked and writhed beneath him, her sensual moans feeding his excitement. He wanted her lips wrapped around his cock, her mouth sucking him to another climax.

Then he felt her hand on his shaft, her touch almost tentative. In fact, her touch felt *too* tentative for someone presenting herself as a major sex kitten playmate.

Her hesitancy confused him. He pulled his mouth away from her just long enough to force out a few words. "Suck my cock." Then he returned to the all too tempting essence that he didn't seem to be able to get enough of. A taste different than any he had previously enjoyed. A taste belonging to a woman who excited him more than anyone he had ever met.

A woman whose identity he didn't even know.

Trish wasn't sure exactly what to do or how to proceed. She had never had a man's cock in her mouth, just as she had never experienced having a man's mouth on her pussy. What his mouth did to her was breathtaking. And then when he had thrust his tongue into her mouth...well, experiencing her own taste for the first time startled her. She wasn't quite sure what to make of it.

Any further thoughts she might have had about this new sensation had quickly evaporated in an incendiary rush when she felt his cock pulse and twitch in orgasm. She had never experienced a man's orgasm in quite that way. Just the memory of the experience propelled her toward yet another climax.

Her chest heaved and her blood raced hot and fast through her veins. Her pussy walls grabbed, contracted and convulsed in orgasmic waves as his mouth brought her to yet another unbelievable orgasm. Never in the twelve years since she lost her virginity in a totally unsatisfactory coupling had she realized sex could be as exciting, breath-taking and incredible as what she was experiencing with Jonathon Rutledge.

His breathless words echoed through her mind...*suck my cock*. A tremor of anxiety attacked her concerns about her lack of experience. His cock looked so large. What if she did it wrong? He'd know she wasn't what she purported to be. He'd know she was a phony. Would he grab off her mask? She had chosen to present herself as someone who had done it all and knew the score. He would surely be suspicious if she didn't do anything.

His tongue thrust in and out of her pussy in several quick jabs, then he laved her swollen clit. Her entire body shuddered as the delicious sensations raced through her. She opened her mouth to cry out in ecstasy, and a moment later, his cock head blocked the sounds.

She wrapped her fingers around his shaft. The extreme hardness surprised her. She tested her tongue against the texture of his cock head, her actions uncertain. The smooth velvety feel excited her already stimulated senses. She closed her lips around this new delight and flicked her tongue across the head several times before actually sucking on it. She had never sucked on any part of a man's anatomy, not even a finger. It was all so new.

And so very exciting.

The texture titillated her awareness, a sensation unlike anything she had ever encountered. A warm feeling filled her, separate from the exquisite orgasmic convulsions that continued to sweep through her body. What his mouth was doing to her was only slightly more exhilarating than having his hard cock in her mouth, an action so forbidden and at the same time so enthralling.

He thrust his hips, and she took more and more of him into her mouth. She tickled her tongue along his rigid shaft, the sensation stimulating her desires. Her mind swirled in a foggy cloud of euphoria. Her entire body coursed with an almost out of control ecstasy.

Without even consciously intending to, she found herself cradling his balls in her hand as she sucked voraciously on his hard sex. A new treat more tantalizing that she could have imagined. Something that sent her ardor into overdrive.

Yet another intense orgasm rippled through her body. There had been so many she lost count. Her pussy muscles grabbed at his tongue as they contracted in rapid succession. Her lips tightened around his shaft and her tongue fluttered across the velvety head as the convulsions totally claimed her. A moment later he pulled his cock out of her mouth, surprising her with the sudden loss of the new treat.

He quickly rolled on another condom, then repositioned himself and penetrated her still convulsing pussy with his throbbing shaft. Long deliberate strokes soon gave way to shorter thrusts as his fervor grew to a peak. He again took control of her mouth, thrusting his tongue into the dark recesses with the same rhythm as his cock delving deep inside her pussy. It didn't take long before the hard shudder of climax ripped through him.

Jonathon slowly rolled off her body, his jet lag and lack of sleep catching up with him. He was definitely all fucked out, at least for the time being. He stretched his tall frame out next to her body and wrapped her in his arms. The frenzy of heated sex had been satiated. He fought to bring his labored breathing under control.

About the only conscious thought he managed to formulate centered around her hesitation, the way she had tentatively approached taking him into her mouth. Even the words she had cried out when he had sucked on her clit. *I've never—*

Had she meant it literally? She had never had a mouth on her pussy before? Combined with her tentative approach to sucking his cock, was it possible this was the first time she had ever participated in oral sex? That she was not the experienced wanton sex goddess she pretended to be?

He ran his fingers along her jaw line, across her shoulder, then tickled them over the swell of her breast. Her soft moan echoed his euphoria. He propped himself up on one elbow, leaned forward and teased her nipple with the tip of his tongue. Everything about her excited him more than any other woman ever had.

Who was this woman who set him on fire, both body and soul? One night was not going to be enough. He suspected a lifetime would not be enough. He tangled his fingers in her hair, but as soon as he touched her mask, she immediately brushed his hand away.

"No. Please don't…"

"You're not going to let me see your face? To know who you are?" At first it had been a tantalizing and exciting game, but now he wanted to know her— who she was, what she thought, what she liked to do. What she liked to do *when she wasn't in bed*. He ran his fingertips across her shoulder, then cupped her breast in his hand. Who was she? Why didn't she want him to know her identity?

An errant thought popped into his mind, accompanied by a quick surge of panic. Was she married? Maybe even the wife of someone he knew? Was that why she insisted on hiding her identity? He grabbed her left hand and stared at her ring finger. No wedding ring, not even any indications that she normally wore a ring on that finger. A wave of relief washed over him. He quickly kissed the inside of her wrist, hoping the gesture would cover what his true intention had been.

He sank back into the softness of the bed, continuing to hold her hand as he clutched it to his chest. He closed his eyes and allowed the softness of her touch to flow through his veins in the same way his blood flowed through his body. They remained quiet for several minutes, one thought constantly circulating through his mind. He wanted to make love to her. Not the frenzied urgency. Not the demands of wanton sex. He wanted slow, sensual, tender, intimate love making. The kind that produced the lasting glow of fulfillment.

He kissed each of her nipples followed by a string of kisses up her throat. He found her mouth. A sweet kiss. A tender kiss. A loving kiss that told of emotional need.

She was a sexy woman he had picked up at a party for the sole purposes of a hot night of recreational fucking. He didn't know who she was or even what her face looked like. How was it possible that his thoughts and feelings had turned from the physical pleasures and a lustful need to an emotional one? What was there about this woman...this *stranger*...that had his thoughts wandering in such a strange direction?

He was tired of living alone. The carefree bachelor

life was never what he strived for. He owned a house, but what he really wanted was a home. A house could never be a home without someone to share his life. Someone to share the highs and the lows, the successes and the failures. Someone to share more than just living space.

Someone to love.

His kiss deepened. He reached for another condom packet and quickly rolled it on his hard cock. He nudged her legs apart, positioned himself between her thighs and slowly entered her.

The sensation was physically exhilarating, but this time it carried an added emotional element, one that both confused and excited him. Her pussy muscles closed in around his hard shaft, encasing him in that hot cocoon he had grown to anticipate. He moved in and out, at first with a deliberately slow pace that spoke of intimacy and feelings as well as passion and physical desire. Each of his down strokes met with her equally enthusiastic upward hip thrust.

At the culmination of each stroke when his hardness was buried all the way inside her, he paused for an instant to fully savor the totality of the moment, the closeness that enveloped him. The pace quickened as the physical need reached out to each of them. He held her tightly in his arms. Long, slow strokes turned to quicker thrusts. Her body writhed beneath him, her cries of ecstasy telling him she was very near to orgasm. Another couple of thrusts, then one last deep plunge and he joined her in the ultimate rapture. He held her body tight against his for several minutes before finally rolling off of her.

His mouth found Trish's again, his kiss as hot as it

Samantha Gentry

had been before only this time without the frenzied urgency attached to it. The kiss was deep, sensual and curled her toes the same way having his hard shaft buried inside her did. She ran her fingers through his thick hair.

No one had ever filled her so completely or penetrated her so deeply. It was almost as if his cock had gone so deep inside her it had struck virgin territory. The exquisite sensations had enveloped her entire body. He was everything she had dreamed he would be. Everything she had fantasized. Everything she had hoped for. And so much more. She had never before experienced a man's mouth on her pussy, but she knew that it certainly wouldn't be the last time. Her body tingled from the intense orgasms he had already given her.

And the night was still young.

The sensation of his strong heartbeat resonated to her fingers. She wanted to take off her mask, to rid herself of the last bit of covering, but she knew she didn't dare. She could never allow Jonathon Rutledge to know the true identity of his mystery lover. If he knew, her embarrassment would be so acute that she would never be able to face him again. She would have to resign from her job before he fired her, a job she loved, working for a man she greatly admired for his business ethics and expertise.

And that wasn't the only thing she admired about him.

Her thoughts turned toward her rapidly escalating concerns about whether she had made a horrible mistake, one she would soon live to regret. One night, that was all she had wanted. One night of unbridled

112

passion with the most incredible, desirable, sexy man she had ever known.

Just one night.

In the last few hours, she had participated in pleasures more intimate, more sensual, more unbelievable and more enthralling than she had ever dreamed possible. And with a man she could easily fall in love with if she gave it half a chance and he offered her even a hint of encouragement. Maybe over the last three years she had already fallen in love with him— gradually, slowly, almost imperceptibly as she maintained her prim and proper business attitude day after day at the office.

He had flirted outrageously with her in the hotel ballroom and assumed she would go to bed with him. He whisked her away to his room for the sole purpose of sex without even knowing who she was or anything about her. On the surface, that would make him an arrogant playboy. But then, she had dressed the part to purposely entice him. The difference was that she knew the person underneath that pretense, a façade no more indicative of the real man than the pirate costume he had chosen for the party.

He pulled her body close to his, holding her tenderly in his arms. It felt so good, so right. It felt like something she wanted to have last forever. She ran her fingers through his hair, then arched her back to thrust her breasts toward his mouth. A moment later his lips were on her nipple, then his tongue licking and teasing the puckered flesh, finally drawing it inside his mouth. He gently suckled, sending a warm wave of contentment through her body. The feeling was totally different from the frenzied urgency of earlier, but every bit as pleasurable.

She stayed in his arms. He gently stroked her hair. Before long his caresses stopped. His slow even breathing told her he had fallen asleep. A little smile of understanding tugged at the corners of her mouth. He had returned from London late Thursday night and had been in the office for a full day of work Friday morning. She didn't know how much sleep he had gotten Friday night, but she knew he had several things on his schedule for Saturday, which precluded his sleeping late on Saturday morning. And then Marty Collins' costume party tonight. There was just no way he could have recovered from his jet lag. And adding several hours of hot, urgent and frenzied sex...he couldn't have stayed awake much longer.

And then he made love to her, beautiful and tender with all the caring anyone could ever wish for.

Her own eyes grew heavy, but she didn't dare fall asleep. She couldn't afford to be in the vulnerable position of having him wake up and remove her mask. A touch of panic tried to take hold. As much as she wanted to spend the entire night with him, leaving now while he was asleep was going to be the most expedient thing to do. It would eliminate any questions, difficulties or awkward moments.

She didn't regret one minute of the intimate time they had spent together, but now that time needed to come to an end. She had to leave as quickly as possible. No matter what she tried to tell herself, and no matter how enthralled she had been with the last several hours, there was no doubt in her mind that the long term effects of her actions would prove her decision to indulge her fantasy had been a very foolish idea.

114

Was she executing a cowardly retreat? Sneaking away while he slept? Should she stay and be accountable for her actions even if she didn't reveal her true identity? She had always been a responsible person, but this was different. Panic grew until it touched every part of her.

Slowly and carefully, she eased out of his arms and edged toward the side of the bed until she could stand. She hurried toward the bathroom and emerged a few minutes later with her dress on and her hair smoothed back. After confirming he was still asleep, she searched for her shoes. She spotted the high heels half hidden under the bed. She moved quietly across the carpeting and picked up her shoes, her plan being to tip toe out of the room.

Then her less than smooth escape totally fell apart when she saw him stir. A combination of extreme panic and stupefying fear stopped her dead in her tracks. If she remained perfectly still and quiet maybe Jonathon would go back to sleep.

He jerked to rigid attention and sat up straight when his gaze landed on her. Total disbelief and confusion covered his features. "Are you going somewhere?"

"It's…it's very late. I didn't want to disturb you."

"So you thought you'd sneak out without even bothering to say good-bye?" A strange combination of alarm and hurt surrounded his words.

"I have to go." She turned and reached for the door security lock.

"Wait. I don't even know who you are. You can't leave, not like this."

He jumped up from the bed, his long legs carrying

him quickly across the room toward her, but before he got there Trish managed to slip out the door and was on her way down the corridor. He was stark naked. No way he could leave the room and come after her.

Chapter Three

Monday morning arrived much too quickly for Trish. Her body still tingled from the night of passion she shared with Jonathon. A night that would live in her memory forever.

But now she had to face him and act as if nothing out of the ordinary had happened, as if their relationship was the same as it had been when they left the office on Friday—that of employer and employee. Her nervousness jumped into high gear the moment she had pulled into the parking lot and saw his car. He had gotten to work early. She hesitated a moment as she took a steadying breath, then opened the door and entered her office. She called to him through the open connecting door to his office.

"Good morning, Mr. Rutledge. You're certainly in early."

He looked up at the sound of her voice and offered a warm though somewhat distracted smile. "Good morning, Miss Andrews. I had several things I needed to take care of, some early morning phone calls to make. Did you have a nice weekend?"

A quick jolt of guilt combined with a heated rush of excitement as the memory flooded through her mind. Her nipples puckered, the sensitive peaks brushing against her bra as a tingle pulsed between her thighs and deep inside her body. "Yes, I did."

She wasn't sure what else to say. Something she hadn't anticipated had suddenly presented itself. A question he had asked her dozens of times, a simple question with no ulterior motive now meant much more than it had in the past. Much more than she was sure he intended it to mean. Nothing was the same as before. What should have been a normal Monday morning had become a journey into uncharted territory. She tried to swallow down her nervousness as she placed her purse in her bottom desk drawer and switched on her computer.

She turned her attention toward the credenza. To her surprise, he had already made coffee. There appeared to be the equivalent of one cup missing from the pot. She poured herself a cup of coffee, then carried the pot into his office and refilled his mug.

The scent of his aftershave attacked her senses. It was the same as he had worn Saturday night. He was dressed casually in jeans and a pullover shirt, the way he usually dressed in the office when he didn't have an important meeting. But what she saw was a perfect specimen of the male physique without the encumbrance of clothes. And most prominent in her vision was his impressive erection standing proud and tall. And oh so very ready.

She moved away from him. Had she stayed there a moment longer she wouldn't have been able to resist the temptation to touch him, to run her fingers through his thick hair, to taste his mouth. To rip off his clothes and ravage him, taking him deep inside her body as she cried out in one exquisite orgasm after another.

She tried to force a calm to her pounding heart and rapid pulse. She turned her attention to the office plants, checking to see if they needed to be watered. "I trust you caught up on your sleep from your London trip."

"I didn't have much of a chance to catch up on my sleep until last night, way too many things to do. Sunday evening was the first time I had a chance to really relax. But I'm feeling fine now, all rested and ready to start a new week."

Jonathon watched for a moment as she filled the pitcher and started to water the plants. *Feeling fine...*that was a laugh. He hadn't felt fine since his mystery lover ran from his room after an incredible night that had continued to play through his mind the rest of the weekend. One painful moment remained burned into his consciousness. The one where he stood frozen to the spot as the hotel room door clicked shut behind her. He had been unable to follow her, totally helpless as she made her escape.

He had no idea who she was or where she had come from. Marty didn't know who she was. How was he ever going to find her? The same strange sense of loss as he felt Saturday night again invaded his reality. He didn't fully understand it, nor could he explain it. But neither could he deny it. Saturday night someone very special had run out of his life. And Jonathon Rutledge, the dynamic and forceful businessman who had no problem juggling several multi-million dollar deals simultaneously, didn't know what to do about it.

All he had to track her down was the hope that someone at Marty Collins' party knew who she was. He had already placed phone calls to Marty and four other people who had been at the party. They all remembered the mysterious woman, but none of them knew who she was. They were going to check with other people who had been at the party. Someone had to know her. She couldn't have just wandered into the hotel wearing a mask in hopes of finding a costume party.

She had to have known about the party in advance. And that meant she had some connection to at least one of the people invited to the party. The slight frown creased his forehead. Or maybe she worked at the hotel in some capacity and knew the ballroom had been booked for a costume party. A sigh of dejection made its way past his lips. Or maybe she knew someone who worked at the hotel. The elusive connection he sought seemed to be moving farther and farther from his grasp.

Somehow he had to find out who she was. A private detective? It was a thought that he filed away in the back of his mind. If nothing else worked out, then it was a possibility. But for now, he had a desk full of work and a serious problem with trying to concentrate on what needed to be done.

He looked up just as Trish finished watering the office plants. "Miss Andrews, could you bring me the file on Premier Associates? I need to do some restructuring on the proposal. I thought we had a done deal, but last Friday's meeting said otherwise."

Trish located the file and brought it to him, thankful for the distraction of business as usual. Somehow she had to get her mind off of Saturday night and back into reality. But it was so much easier said than done. Every time she got within fifteen feet of him a tingle of excitement rippled across her skin, her pulse raced and a throbbing need between her legs dampened the crotch of her panties.

She had convinced herself that one night was all she wanted. One night of unbridled passion would be enough. She now knew she had only been kidding herself. She had to have another night with him, but how? The costume party had been a perfect setting for a mysterious meeting with total anonymity. What could she come up with that would duplicate those circumstances? Something that would entice him yet assure her anonymity?

The more she thought about it, the more determined she became to somehow orchestrate another night of passion with the incredibly sexy Jonathon Rutledge. Would that be pushing her luck one step too far?

She dismissed the negative thought. The rest of the work day progressed in a busy manner, leaving her little time to speculate and day dream. But as soon as she arrived home, she made it the number one item for the evening.

By the time she went to bed, Trish Andrews had come up with a plan. There was only one little hitch. In order to implement her plan, she would have to let Jonathon know that his mystery lover knew who he was. It would no longer be two strangers at an accidental meeting. Would he go along with her plan without knowing her identity? It was a chance she would take. A chance she *needed* to take.

She purchased a box of lacy ultra-feminine stationery in a passionate pink color. She wrote him a note, using a script font on her computer so he wouldn't recognize the handwriting. She had given a lot of thought to the exact wording of the note. She didn't want it to sound pornographic, but she definitely wanted to arouse him.

My Dear Captain Sparrow: My body has been on

fire since our meeting. I ache for more of your touch. There's so much left for us to explore. I want to see you this Saturday to continue where we left off, including wearing the same costumes we wore when we shared that marvelous night of passion. I've reserved room sixty-nine at the Bayfront Inn on Old Shoreline Road. I'll be so disappointed if you reject my invitation. I'll be waiting for you at seven o'clock. Until then...

She signed the note *The Lady In Red*, sprayed the envelope with a hint of the special perfume she had worn that night and mailed it on her way to work the next morning. She knew it would be delivered the following day.

A nervous energy coiled inside Trish for the rest of that day. Jonathon appeared busy, but she couldn't help notice that he also seemed distracted from time to time. He obviously had something on his mind other than work. She hoped it was the memory of his mystery lover, that their night of wild abandon was as profound for him as it had been for her. She would soon know the answer, but would it be the answer she wanted to hear?

By the next morning her nervous energy had progressed to full blown anxiety. She remained on pins and needles until the morning mail arrived. She immediately spotted the passionate pink envelope that clearly stated *personal and confidential* next to his name and address. After opening the rest of the mail as she normally would, she carried it into his office and placed it on his desk.

He looked up at her, but before he could say anything she handed him the envelope. "This one was marked personal. It doesn't have a return address. Do you want me to have security check it out?"

Jonathon caught a hint of the fragrance his mystery lover had worn. Could it possibly be a note from her? But how could that be? How would she know who to send it to? And where?

"Uh…no need, Miss Andrews. I'm sure it isn't anything that requires the attention of the security department." He took the envelope and stared at it for a moment before returning his attention to his administrative assistant. She seemed to be waiting for something. "Is there anything else, Miss Andrews?"

"Oh…no, nothing."

He watched as she left, then closed his office door so he could turn his full attention to the mysterious envelope. He inhaled the fragrance. It was definitely the same perfume. An image of a stunning body immediately filled his mind followed closely by a hard jolt of heated lust. His cock twitched as the memory of that incredible night came rushing back at him, of the way his cock felt buried deep inside her hot pussy, of the taste uniquely hers. His hand trembled slightly as he opened the envelope and read the note.

Two conflicting emotions immediately clashed inside him, each battling for dominance. His stiffening cock and emotions won out over his intellectual concerns. Maybe fate had stepped in to give him another opportunity to identify his mystery lover. He couldn't allow the opportunity to get away, but he needed to take some precautions. She knew who he was, but he didn't have a clue about her other than no one else had made him throb with hot need the way she did. He glanced at the closed door again, making sure no one could hear him. Then he reached for his phone.

Trish saw the light go on showing Jonathon's line

was in use. Was it a business call or something to do with her note? It was too late to take it back. She had initiated phase two and had to see it through.

The rest of the week seemed to crawl by. The end of the work day on Friday finally arrived. Jonathon hadn't made any mention of the pink envelope, and Trish couldn't ask him about it without arousing suspicion. Had he thrown it away in disgust? Had he dismissed it as a joke? Did he plan to be at the inn at seven o'clock? Had she done a totally stupid thing in sending the note?

Her original plan had been for one night of passion. She slowly shook her head. One night wasn't enough. Would two nights be enough? She instinctively knew the answer. A hundred nights wouldn't be enough. A thousand nights wouldn't be enough. She would never have her fill of Jonathon Rutledge. The rest of her life would be spent wanting more.

Her entire body tingled with the need to have him embedded deep inside her. To feel the thrust of his rock hard shaft moving in and out. To once again experience that incredible surge of rapture when he sucked her clit into his mouth. And in a little over twenty-four hours she would hopefully know that excitement again.

****

Jonathon pulled his car into the parking lot of the Bayfront Inn. He had dressed in the wide collared shirt with dark vest, sash, leather belt with large buckle and pirate boots he had worn to the party. The buccaneer hat and headwrap with the attached beaded braids rested on the passenger seat.

He parked, then sat in his car for a minute before making any effort to open the door. While he appreciated her flair and the obvious message in booking room sixty-nine, he couldn't help but wonder if he was about to make a colossal mistake. He closed his eyes and reveled in the memory of the way her hot tight pussy closed in around his cock, her enthusiastic response, her delicious taste exploding in his mouth. He opened his car door. He wanted another night with his mystery lover.

And he had to find out who she was.

He walked the short distance from where he had parked to her room and knocked on the door. It slowly swung open. The sight that greeted him had his cock standing tall and screaming for immediate attention. Everything that had so captured his attention at the costume party again assaulted his senses. And this time there was the added knowledge of exactly what he would find underneath that sexy red dress—what it looked like, how it tasted and how it made him feel.

A long, low whistle escaped his lips. "Oh, yes, my sexy beauty. Last Saturday was a warm up. Tonight will definitely be a night to remember."

"You're not wearing all your costume." A hint of disappointment surrounded her words.

"Since you saw me without my mask last week and obviously know who I am, I didn't see any reason to don the full regalia. You, however, are still a complete mystery."

She stepped aside, allowing him entry to the room. "Please come in, Captain Sparrow. I'm delighted that you decided to accept my invitation."

"I'm altering your plans." Even with her mask covering most of her face, he could see the apprehension dart through her eyes. He didn't know what was behind any of this other than the obvious incredible sex, but he wasn't about to allow a stranger to predetermine where they would have their tryst. If there was some sort of ulterior motive behind this, perhaps a hidden camera or something of that sort, he at least wanted control of the place where he intended to spend the entire night fucking his mystery lover. "I've taken the liberty of reserving a different room for us just a short walk from this one."

A quick moment of panic hit Trish. This was not the way she had intended for the evening to progress. Was her hoped for night of passion beginning to self-destruct right before her eyes? Then he flashed that incredibly sexy smile and her insides melted. He held out his hand toward her and she accepted it.

He quickly glanced around the inside of the room. "Is there anything here you need to take with you?"

As she had done a week ago, everything was in the trunk of her car and the doors could be unlocked by the keypad so she didn't need a key. She finally shook her head when she couldn't force out any words. Just the feel of his hand grasping hers had her clit tingling in anticipation.

He led her to a room five doors away from the one she had booked. As soon as he unlocked the door and stepped aside for her to enter, she saw why he had chosen it. It was no ordinary room.

She had known the caveman room at the inn existed, but had never seen it. Everything about it screamed unbridled hot passion from the round king size bed to the rock walls, the waterfall shower enclosure in the bathroom, the hot tub in front of the wood burning fireplace. The ice bucket containing a bottle of champagne and two glasses next to the bed didn't escape her attention, either.

As he had done before, Jonathon put out the *Do Not Disturb* sign and set the security lock. Then he turned toward her and placed his hands on her shoulders. "Please take off your mask. I want to see your face."

She brushed his hand aside. "No. As we agreed last time, no—"

"Not so fast. Last time we also agreed to no names, just two strangers indulging in a fantasy night of passion. Well, it seems that those rules no longer apply. You saw my face, and then I found that you knew my name and where to reach me. Doesn't it seem a little unfair that you won't allow me to see your face?"

"No…not yet." At that moment, she knew beyond a shadow of a doubt she had made a huge mistake. If he was determined to remove her mask, there was absolutely nothing she could do to prevent it. Would he honor her request? She held her breath, waiting to see what he would do.

"All right." He flashed a grin. "For the time being."

Just the sight of that devastatingly sexy smile puckered her nipples, the sensation running all the way down to her already wet pussy. Then his next words told her just how incredible it was going to be.

"Why don't you slip out of that gown? I've got a hunger gnawing at me that I know you can satisfy."

Conversation time was over. As captivating as she was in that red dress, Jonathon wanted her naked on the bed. His cock had been standing at rigid attention from the moment he set eyes on her when she opened the door of the other room.

He extended a confident smile in an attempt to cover his concerns. "I'll get rid of my clothes, and we'll see if we can find something better to do than stand here staring at each other."

He pulled off his boots and unbuttoned his shirt, but before taking it off, he opened the champagne and poured two glasses. He handed one to her. When she took it from his hand, he noticed the delicate gold filigree ring she wore on her little finger. It suited her. Beautiful on the surface, yet composed of an intricate pattern too complex to immediately unravel. Just like her…wanton sex kitten or a woman with limited experience pretending to be something she wasn't?

He clinked his glass against hers in the form of a toast. "Here's to another incredible night."

She smiled. "Yes, another incredible night."

"This time I've had a good night's sleep. No jet lag. No exhaustion to detract from a night of indulging all sort of uninhibited fun. We can fuck until dawn. In fact, we can fuck all day Sunday or until we dissolve into a puddle of total collapse—whichever happens first."

They sipped their champagne as they gazed into each other's eyes. Looks of heated desire promising untold pleasures silently passed between them. Once again there was something familiar about her eyes and her mouth, but he couldn't place it.

Then to Jonathon's delight, his mystery lover assumed control of the moment. She took the empty glass from his hand and set it on the night stand next to her empty glass. Then she pushed him back until he fell onto the bed with his legs dangling over the edge. After slowly lowering his zipper, she reached inside his pants and fondled his balls. The glow in the depth of her eyes immediately told him he was going to enjoy whatever she had in mind. The notion of being on the receiving end of her unknown intentions was a definite turn on.

He raised his hips so she could pull off his pants and briefs. His cock sprang free, once again standing tall and proud. And definitely primed for action. Where she had seemed unsure about several things last week, this week she aggressively took the initiative. He didn't know what happened during the ensuing week, but whatever it was had his complete approval.

He tossed his shirt on the floor next to his pants and pulled off his socks, all the while watching with fascination as she did a modified striptease for him. This time there was nothing on under the dress. As sexy and exciting as the sight of the red garter belt and sheer black stockings had been, the sight of her totally nude body with the blonde curls decorating her pussy brought a low growl up from the very depths of his primal needs. This time he already knew the many pleasures and intense rapture that existed between those sleek thighs.

Jonathon may have altered her original plans by changing the location of their rendezvous, but Trish intended to put any and all of her normal inhibitions aside and allow her secret desires to run rampant. She would put to use the new things he had introduced her to the previous week and be the sexy woman she had always dreamed of being. Once her mind let go of her conservative upbringing, bolstered by the security of her anonymity, she allowed her earthy wild desires to take over.

She ran her hands across the hard planes of his

chest, the feel of his bare skin sending waves of need crashing through her body and exciting her senses. She had given it a lot of thought over the last couple of days. She wanted to be on top, to experience what that type of control felt like. To know how much deeper inside her his impressive cock would reach.

Before mounting him and allowing her hungry pussy to sink onto his beautiful hard shaft, she had to taste him. The memory of his cock inside her mouth, the sensation of her tongue swirling around the head and along his shaft, had tantalized her senses. And even more exciting was the unforgettable first time he flicked his tongue across her clit, then drew it into his mouth. She wanted to know that incendiary moment again, and this time she had the knowledge and confidence to take full advantage of this new and exciting treat.

"In honor of the room number that I booked..." She turned around and stretched out along the length of his torso with his rigid shaft bobbing in front of her mouth and her muff hovering just above his face. Each ragged breath he expelled against her tender pussy lips sent a delicious tingle of anticipation rippling through her body. She cradled his balls, the texture of the sac feeding into her excitement. This time she knew what was going to happen and what she wanted, the incredible orgasms that would once again be hers. Just the thought had her juices flowing.

She placed a tender kiss on the very tip of his cock, then licked the drop of salty pre-cum. She trailed her tongue up and down his hard length before taking the head into her mouth. His husky groan of pleasure fed into the quivering delight coursing inside her.

A moment later, his mouth was on her pussy,

sending a hard jolt of ecstasy ricocheting through her body, touching every nerve ending she possessed. She ground her sex against his mouth seeking more and more. Her chest heaved as she gasped for breath. She wrapped her hand around his thick shaft, pumping in tandem with his cock sliding in and out of her mouth. The night had just started and already her pussy was on fire, convulsing in hard contractions of rapture as the intense orgasm convulsed through her body.

An orgasm that seemed to go on and on. An orgasm that wouldn't stop. She had never experienced anything like it. Wave after wave crashed through her body. Her mind whirled out of control. She couldn't think. All she could do was savor the intensity of the exquisite sensations while craving more.

Jonathon grabbed the rounded globes of her bottom, kneading the firm flesh with his fingers. He closed his eyes and inhaled deeply. The tantalizing fragrance of her sex filled his lungs and charged his arousal. Where last week she had been tentative about sucking his cock, this week she eagerly embraced it. Her tongue…her mouth…the rhythm of her sucking…she quickly drove him to the edge—much quicker than he wanted. He needed to slow her down but couldn't bring himself to the point where he would back away from her enthusiastic attentions.

He placed a kiss on her clit, then laved the flat of his tongue across her pussy lips. Her delicious taste exploded in his mouth, a taste he vividly remembered and had craved all week. He felt her gasp as much as heard it. A moment later he drew her engorged clit fully into his mouth and teased it with his tongue before sucking on the delicate treat.

Jonathon bucked his hips upward as her lips tightened around his shaft. If this was an indication of how the night was going to progress, he seriously doubted that he would live to see the dawn. But it was one hell of a way to go, being fucked to death by an incredibly sexy and beautiful woman. They could put it on his tombstone—*death by orgasm, he died with a smile on his face.*

He thrust his tongue as far into her pussy as he could and seductively wiggled it so that it touched her everywhere. He continued to stimulate her clit with his fingers. His balls tightened and pulled up. He had to get her mouth off his cock before he totally lost it. But his next breath told him it was too late.

His head jerked back into the pillow. His release shuddered deep inside him as hard spasms raced through his body and spurts of semen shot into her mouth.

She continued to suck his spent organ with the type of intensity that could only be driven by her own highly aroused state. To his surprise and delight, his mystery lover had him hard and primed for action in a matter of minutes. He gasped for air, needing the oxygen but not wanting to abandon the delicious treat so temptingly close to his mouth. Once again he flicked the tip of his tongue against her engorged clit relishing her moans of pleasure as she continued to administer to his cock.

Trish couldn't believe her totally wanton behavior, but it felt so good to let go of any and all inhibitions. Carnal pleasure was the rule for the night. If it promised to send orgasmic waves through her body, then she wanted to do it. She wanted to experience all she could. And she wanted to experience it with Jonathon

Rutledge.

Her pussy continued to quiver and convulse with each flick of his tongue. His cock was once again hard, thick and long. She felt the life pulse through it, then allowed his length to slip from her mouth.

She quickly turned around and straddled his hips. As she fought to catch her breath, he grabbed a packet, ripped it open and rolled the condom on his stiff shaft. A lascivious grin tugged at his mouth, the same mouth that had so thoroughly and deliciously ravaged her most intimate of places sending her into a series of glorious orgasms. Lust and primal need burned in the depths of his eyes. Her tautly puckered nipples ached with a need to be touched. As if reading her mind, he cupped her breasts in his hands and pulled her forward until he was able to draw one of the hard buds into his mouth.

She closed her eyes and purred softly as he suckled. It was a warm sensation that conveyed contentment, but she wanted more. She wanted his magnificent cock buried deep inside her, as deep as it could go.

Without disturbing the wonderful sensation his suckling provided, she wrapped her hand around his shaft and guided his hard sex to her pussy. Slowly...oh, so slowly...she inched her way down onto his rigid cock. His girth stretched and filled her, his length going farther and farther until it found the deepest reaches of her tunnel. His coarse thatch of pubic hair tickled her highly stimulated clit.

The depth of his penetration, her clit rubbing against him—never had she imagined anything could be so incredible. Her pussy walls grabbed his shaft, the contractions beginning the moment she started to rock back and forth. Once again the sensations washed over her, elevating her to a level of rapture more powerful than anything she had ever known.

The night of pleasure continued, the air thick with a heady mixture of the aroma and sounds of sex. Trish wanted to get rid of her mask. It was in the way and had almost come off during one particularly energetic coupling. But she didn't dare. No matter how fogged her mind became, no matter how scattered her thoughts, no matter how delicious the exquisite pleasure, she did not lose sight of the one absolute—under no circumstances could she allow him to know her identity. Was there any way she would be able to lure him to a third Saturday night of uninhibited hot sex and still be able to preserve her anonymity?

Her thoughts were interrupted when he urged her to roll onto her stomach, pull her legs up and spread them wide apart. A tremor of anxiety darted through her, putting a momentary damper on her heightened state of arousal. She wasn't sure what he planned.

She heard him rip open the condom packet, then a moment later his cock head probed at her pussy mouth from behind. He reached around her and expertly manipulated her throbbing clit with his fingers, again propelling her toward the ongoing orgasms that had consumed her the entire evening.

He shoved into her until he had his cock embedded all the way inside her hot wet tunnel. The angle, the direction, having him enter her from behind provided a whole new sensory arena to explore. She automatically pushed back against him in response, wiggling her ass to show her delight and excitement.

He thrust in and out with long sure strokes, which

quickly became short hard jabs as he rushed toward his release. He gave up all pretense of trying to make it last. Her pussy muscles grabbed and squeezed his shaft as her orgasmic contractions continued to claim her. A moment later, his body shuddered. He took one last hard plunge to bury his cock deep inside her. He reached around and grabbed her breasts as he fell forward against her, his chest heaving and his heart pounding.

The spasms rippled through his body. He gulped in several deep breaths. He finally managed to pull his spent cock out of her tight pussy then collapsed back on the bed. He forced the words that came out in a husky whisper. "My sexy vixen...I think we need to take a breather and have some champagne."

After a few minutes of rest, Jonathon disposed of the used condoms and condom wrappers, each one evoking memories of sex so intense it should have scorched the sheets. The time had arrived for cuddling, softness, gentle play and perhaps a renewed attempt to discover who she was.

He opened another bottle of chilled champagne and poured two glasses. He had never felt so totally drained and at the same time so energized and wanting more. He stood next to the bed admiring the sexy frame stretched out seductively on the rumpled sheets. It was a time for cuddling, but most certainly not the end of the night.

He sat on the bed with his back resting against the headboard and his legs stretched out in front of him. She immediately scooted up next to him. He put his arm around her shoulder and stroked her hair. They sipped their champagne in silence, each enjoying the quiet moments of reflection. He refilled their glasses. They nestled together in intimate closeness, an unconscious emotional bonding.

The empty bottle rested in the ice bucket. She snuggled next to him. He skimmed his fingers lightly across the creamy texture of her skin. He brushed her hair back and placed a soft kiss on the side of her neck. For the first time he noticed the tiny heart-shaped birthmark behind her ear. It was as delicate as the essence of her being.

He wanted to make love to her as he had the previous Saturday night. Tender, gentle, caring lovemaking different than frenzied, torrid sex. He wanted to recapture that emotional connection. The one that spoke of commitment, a home, a family—happily ever after. What was there about this woman, this mysterious stranger, that had his thoughts again heading in that direction?

His mouth closed over hers in a loving kiss, an emotional kiss. He ran his hand down the length of her back and across the perfect roundness of her ass as he pulled her body tighter against his. He reveled in the warmth of her closeness, the sensation of her bare skin touching his.

Her breathing increased as his kiss deepened. He turned her onto her back where she sank into the softness of the bed, his body partially covering hers. He slipped his hand between her legs, tickling his fingers up the inside of her thigh until he reached the softness of the feathery curls nestled between her legs. He slowly inserted one finger between her pussy lips and into the moist heat of her body. She moaned softly in his ear, the sound pushing his arousal to a higher level.

He quickly sheathed his cock with another condom and smoothly entered her.

Her long blonde hair flared out across the pillow in wild disarray, giving her an earthy seductive appearance. He saw the passion burning in her eyes. If only he could see her face. She had him encased in that hot tight sheath, her pussy muscles doing incredible things to him that he couldn't begin to describe. All he knew for sure was that he could spend a lifetime and never find anyone who satisfied all his desires the way she did. And if they didn't do anything more for the rest of the night than what they were doing right now, he knew he could die a happy and *very* satisfied man.

He moved smoothly in and out of her tight, wet sheath, each thrust conveying tender feelings. Their mutual climax exploded in sexual release accompanied by an equally potent emotional bonding. He continued to hold her in his arms as he delicately stroked her skin and hair.

Jonathon wasn't sure what to do. At some point the night had to end. At some point they would leave the inn and go their separate ways. And once again he would be left with a strange emptiness and no idea of how to find his mysterious lover. Hot, sexy, wanton, earthy—she was all those things. Tender, soft, loving—she was also all those things. He didn't want to lose her. He reached for her mask.

She quickly scooted out of his reach before he could unmask her. "No."

He turned on his side and propped himself up on one elbow. "Why not? What are you hiding? Are you someone I know? Will I immediately recognize you without your mask? Let me see your face. Let me know who you are."

"I...I can't. Please don't ask me any more questions."

He couldn't see her face, but he saw the pleading in her eyes. It was almost a look of panic. Who was she? What would the implications be if he knew her identity? What was there that made her so fearful?

He leaned toward her, placed a tender kiss on her lips, then slid out of bed. "I'll be right back."

Trish's gaze followed his retreating form until he closed the bathroom door. She hadn't been sure a week ago, but now there was no doubt. Somewhere over the last three years, she had fallen in love with Jonathon Rutledge.

As much as the beauty of their lovemaking would remain in her consciousness, she couldn't continue to work for him. She knew she wouldn't be able to handle day to day contact with this man, knowing it would always be a hands off business relationship. Maybe she could have before, but not now. Not after experiencing the torrid passion that existed between them. A bittersweet tremor shivered through her body. The euphoria of a moment earlier had suddenly turned to sadness.

For right now, she needed to leave the room and there was the only way she would be able to do it without creating a problem. After quickly shrugging into her dress, she searched for her shoes, finally spotting them under the edge of the bed. She started toward them, moving quickly but quietly across the carpeting.

"Damn!" She immediately clamped her hand over her mouth.

Her little toe throbbed painfully. *Damn bed frame leg.* It was a complication she definitely didn't need. She lifted her foot in the air and wrapped her hand around her injured toe while attempting to maintain balance on the other foot. Her ankle twisted under her. She felt it, but was helpless to prevent the fall that sent her sprawling on the floor.

Double damn, what else can go wrong? I have to get out of here.

She struggled to her feet, carefully trying to protect her stubbed toe on one foot while favoring her painful ankle on the other leg. Then her less than smooth escape totally fell apart when the bathroom door opened.

Jonathon's eyes widened in shock. "Are you going somewhere?" He pointed to her foot as she edged toward the door. "What happened?"

"I...uh, stubbed my toe on the bed frame leg and then twisted my ankle when I fell." She took another step closer to the door.

"So, it's just like last week. You're sneaking out, running away without even saying good-bye."

The look of disappointment and hurt on his face grabbed at her, but she knew she had to steel herself against the emotions. A quick glance at her shoes told her she would never be able to retrieve them and make it out the door without him pulling off her mask.

She unlocked the safety and flung open the door. Ignoring the pain in her ankle, she fled out into the night.

Chapter Four

As with the previous week, Trish was surprised to see Jonathon's car in the parking lot when she arrived at work Monday morning. She climbed out of her car, testing to see how much weight she could put on her sprained ankle without needing to favor it. She had hoped to already be in the office and at her desk when he arrived. She had wrapped her ankle in a flesh colored support bandage and had chosen to wear slacks and low heeled shoes in an attempt to hide the sprain. She took a couple of steps and quickly realized she was not going to be able to walk without a slight limp no matter how much she tried to ignore the pain.

A few minutes later, she entered the office and followed her usual Monday morning routine. "Good morning, Mr. Rutledge. Did you have a nice weekend?"

He returned her greeting from the confines of his office. "Good morning, Miss Andrews. Yes, thank you. And you?"

"Just a quiet weekend. I caught up on some chores and ran errands. Nothing special." *Nothing special—no, nothing special at all other than the hottest sex of my life with the most incredible man alive. A man I think I've fallen in love with.*

She made coffee, turned on her computer and prepared for the day's work. As soon as the coffee was ready, she filled his mug and carried it into his office.

Even though she made a valiant attempt, she could not help but favor her ankle a little bit. Hopefully he wouldn't notice. The next item on her normal Monday morning routine was to water the plants in his office. She set the coffee mug on his desk.

He looked up and offered a distracted smile. "Thank you, Miss Andrews."

Jonathon took a sip of coffee, then another. He had spent a very restless night going over the final moments of his time with his mystery lover. Once again he had stood there stark naked, unable to follow her outside the room. And as before he was filled with the sensation that someone very special had just run out of his life. Then he spotted her shoes. He had been left with a clue. A slim lead, but at least it was something.

He had been in his office since six o'clock that morning going over lists of everyone he knew, both personal and business. He couldn't come up with anyone who matched the description of his mysterious lover—not a woman he had dated nor even the wife of any of his most obscure business contacts. He had finally resorted to looking up private detectives in the phone book.

Unlike last week, this time he had a lead. Actually two leads. In addition to her shoes, there was the room she had booked at the Bayfront Inn. If she paid with a credit card, that was a definite lead to follow. Even if she paid cash in advance, she would need to do that in person, which meant someone saw her face. One way or the other, he was determined to find out exactly who she was.

He glanced down at the pair of red high heels on the floor next to his desk. He had not bothered to really inspect them. If only he felt confident that he would be as lucky as Prince Charming in tracking down his Cinderella after she had run away from the ball, leaving her shoe behind.

An abstract thought entered his mind. Cinderella had pretended to be a princess so she could pass herself off as someone other than who she really was, someone she believed the prince would find acceptable, someone of the prince's peer group. Could his Cinderella be someone other than who she had pretended to be? Someone who insisted on keeping her mask on because he would recognize her if he saw her face even if he didn't know her name? Perhaps someone he came in contact with during the course of his business day? Someone who—

He watched Trish walk across the office, carrying the pitcher to water the plants. Something was different. She was walking with a very slight limp. He looked closer, taking note of her wrapped ankle in spite of the fact that she was wearing pants rather than a skirt.

He gestured toward her foot. "You injured yourself, Miss Andrews?"

"Uh...yes, I took a misstep off a curb in the grocery store parking lot yesterday afternoon and twisted my ankle. It's not bad. I'm sure it will be fine in a day or two." She resumed watering the plants.

Jonathon picked up the high heels from the floor, turning them to inspect the soles. They were almost brand new. He set them on his desk. Had they been purchased specifically for the party to go with that sexy red dress, then only worn again the following Saturday night? Too many questions. Too many pieces of the puzzle. Everything began to bounce around inside his head, pieces floating in the air looking for a place to settle, a pattern to fit into.

Was his lady in red someone sent by one of his competitors to trap him in some way? Maneuver him into a compromising position? A night of sex wouldn't do that. Two nights of sex wouldn't do it, either. After all, he wasn't married or even engaged. It might cause a little bit of embarrassment for him, but nothing more.

Business secrets? Neither one of them ever mentioned anything having to do with business, his or hers. In fact, there hadn't been that much conversation of any kind. He had already confirmed that she hadn't been wearing a wedding ring nor did she normally wear a ring on that finger. Yet she somehow knew him, not only his name but where to find him.

Trish finished watering the plants, but as she turned toward the door her gaze landed on the high heels resting on his desk, the ones that hadn't been there a couple of minutes ago. The ones she left in the room at the inn as she made her hasty departure. Her breath froze in her lungs. Panic consumed her to the point she could barely think. She felt light-headed.

Had he discovered her identity? Figured out that she was the mystery woman? Was he simply biding his time until the right moment presented itself for him to confront her? Had he placed the shoes on his desk in hopes that they would intimidate her into confessing? Was he simply toying with her?

She tried to take in a deep breath to break the tightness pulling across her chest. *Stay calm...stay calm...breathe slowly.*

Jonathon rose from his chair and came out from behind his desk. "Are you all right, Miss Andrews?

You look pale as a ghost."

"I'm—I'm fine. Really."

He grabbed her arm and steered her toward the couch. "Sit down. I'll get you a glass of water."

He rushed to the bar in the corner of his large office, filled a glass with ice and water, then returned. "Here, have a drink of this. Then lean back and rest for a bit."

As she took the glass from him, he noticed the ring she wore on her little finger of her left hand. He had been aware she always wore a ring but had never paid any attention to it. Until now. He had seen it before, the delicate filigree pattern. It was the same ring worn by his mystery lover.

A thought too preposterous to be true started to take hold in his mind. Could it be? Was it even remotely possible? Did he really want to know?

He tilted his head and turned his gaze to the spot behind her ear. The spot where he had noticed the tiny heart shaped birthmark on his mystery lover. He closed his eyes as he forced a calm to his breathing. Then he slowly opened them and focused on the spot, on the delicate heart shaped birthmark behind Miss Andrews' ear.

The blue eyes and sensual mouth, the only part of her face that had been visible around the mask, he now knew where he had seen them before. They had been in front of him for the last three years, only he had never noticed. Miss Andrews—tailored, all business, efficient with her hair pulled back in that tight bun.

Trish Andrews, who had turned his life upside down and inside out in one night, then confirmed it with a second night of unbridled passion. The hottest sex and most tender lovemaking he had ever shared with a woman.

A quick surge of panic told him exactly how out of control he felt at that moment. He didn't know what to do or how to proceed. He couldn't simply continue with his business day as if nothing had happened.

He would never again be able to look at her and see only his efficient administrative assistant without also seeing the blonde curls feathered across her mound. Without seeing the passion glowing in the depths of her blue eyes. Without seeing her perfect breasts capped with the deliciously puckered nipples. Without knowing her unique taste and the way it continued to linger in his senses. Without remembering the way her tight pussy walls encased his cock in a hot wet cocoon that sent exquisite waves of rapture crashing through his body.

Without reliving the two most incredible nights he had ever experienced.

They had to talk about this, but she had gone to great lengths to make sure he didn't know she was his mystery lover. He couldn't simply blurt it out and take a chance on humiliating her. What if she walked away from him again? And this time permanently? He couldn't allow that to happen.

"Are you feeling better?" He tried to force a calm, casual timbre to his voice. To sound normal. But normal no longer existed. He wanted to take the pins from her hair and let it fall around her shoulders, to caress the creamy smooth texture of her skin. To kiss her delicious mouth. To taste every inch of her.

And so much more.

"Yes, thank you."

She glanced up as she handed him the water glass,

but didn't make eye contact. She looked as uncertain as he felt. "Your, uh, ankle? Are you sure it's okay? Did you go to the doctor or the emergency room?"

"No, there wasn't any need to. It's just a simple sprain."

He kneeled down beside her and carefully slipped her shoe off her foot. He pressed gently on her ankle. "Does this hurt?"

"Just a little twinge. It's nothing—really. Please don't concern yourself."

Trish was scared. Did he know or was it her guilty conscience leading her astray? She had been handling everything okay until he escorted her to the couch. The moment he touched her was almost too much. And then he held her calf as he removed her shoe. Regardless of his good intentions and genuine concern as employer to employee, for her it was an intimate gesture that brought back every intense ripple of orgasmic delight she had experienced with him.

But it was immediately followed by a rush of foreboding. She had done a very stupid thing and now she was going to have to pay for it. If only she could turn back the clock.

No. That was not what she wanted. The two nights would live in her memory and in her heart as the most exciting time of her life. But the apparent consequences were something she hadn't adequately prepared for. She squeezed her eyes shut. Maybe if she concentrated hard enough it would all go away.

But rather than the memories being banished, an image of his naked body popped into her mind. Just the sight of his hard erection standing tall and ready sent a gush that dampened the crotch of her panties. Her nipples puckered into taut peaks, the sensitive buds rubbing against the lacy fabric of her bra. A tingle of excitement hummed between her legs, a need that demanded the type of attention her vibrator could never satisfy. The kind of attention that only Jonathon Rutledge could provide.

Her thoughts were interrupted when he again grasped her calf and slid the shoe on her foot.

"Well, it seems to be a perfect fit. What do you think…Cinderella?"

Her eyes opened with startled alarm. She looked down at her foot, at the red high heel that was, indeed, a perfect fit. She closed her eyes again and buried her face in her hands. She couldn't bear to look at him, to see the contempt and disgust on his face. A sick churning in the pit of her stomach tried to work its way up her throat. There was no way she could deny anything. It was over.

There was nothing left for her to do except resign before he fired her.

She lowered her hands, but she still could not look at him. "I offer you my sincere apologies, Mr. Rutledge. You will, of course, have my immediate resignation along with my promise to not say or do anything that will compromise your reputation or further embarrass or humiliate you."

She felt his weight sink down on the couch next to her. Then there was a long moment of silence. Full-blown anxiety raced through her body, touching every corner of her consciousness. She couldn't stand it any longer. She glanced at him, and what she saw truly stunned her. No contempt, no disgust, no condemnation. She saw only tenderness and caring...and confusion.

"I don't understand, Miss Andrews. Why did you do it?"

"I..." Trish quickly averted her eyes, choosing to stare at the pattern on the carpeting. She didn't know what to say or how to answer his question. She shook her head. "It doesn't matter anymore. As I said, you'll have my resignation immediately."

"I'm afraid I have to disagree with you. It *does* matter. I want to know. What prompted you to go to such lengths? To perpetuate such an elaborate deception?"

"It's—I just wanted one night—"

"One night?"

"One night that became two nights—"

"For three years you've been in my office five days a week, and you never let on—I never suspected..." He drew in a deep breath, held it for several seconds, then slowly exhaled. "I'm not sure what to say, Miss Andrews."

"You don't need to say anything. What I did was inexcusable. You don't need to ask for my resignation. I'll have it on your desk within the quarter hour."

Jonathon placed his fingertips under her chin and gently lifted until he could look into her eyes. They were the same eyes that had been so filled with fire and heated passion. Now he saw anxiety and trepidation, and it upset him. It also left him slightly bewildered. The very special woman who he thought he had lost turned out to be someone he knew well...yet apparently didn't know at all. He wanted to see the fire of passion again, to know the heat of their combined desires.

"I won't be asking for your resignation."

She wrinkled her brow in confusion. "I don't understand."

"Well, Miss Andrews…" He plucked the pins from her hair until it fell loose to her shoulders. "I was about to ask for something, but it wasn't your resignation."

The mesmerizing control of his stare, combined with the way he had undone her hair, left Trish speechless. She wasn't sure what was happening, but she knew his closeness robbed her of the ability to muster even a mild protest.

He reached for the top button of her blouse and slowly unfastened it. Then the next and the next. Her insides quivered with a combination of excitement and anxiety. She finally forced herself to move. She placed her hand on top of his, stopping him before he unfastened the next button.

"Please don't, Mr. Rutledge—"

"I think in light of everything that's happened, it would be okay if we dropped the formalities…Trish." Jonathon closed his eyes for a moment. The perfect breasts with the deliciously puckered nipples, the incredible body that could drive any grown man to distraction, the blonde curls decorating the entrance to a treasure worth fighting for. And all of it topped by a beautiful face he saw every day yet never really noticed.

He pulled her into his embrace. Oddly enough, it was not the call of hot sex that propelled his actions. She felt good in his arms. It all felt right. Could it be that he had finally found what had been missing from his life?

He lowered his mouth to hers. The spark of desire ignited the moment their lips came in contact. But again, the spark was not one demanding the pleasures he knew her body held. It was a spark of emotional need, a desire for closeness.

Trish wrapped her arms around his neck, melted into his embrace and fully responded to his kiss. The kiss deepened. He twined his tongue with hers in a sensual mating that fed his emotional desires as much as his physical ones. His thoughts filled with the two times they had made tender love, the emotionally fulfilling intimacy. That's what he wanted at the moment. But he couldn't assume she wanted the same thing.

He reluctantly broke the kiss, but continued to hold her in his arms. "I didn't think I'd ever see you again. I've been exploring every avenue I could think of in hopes of finding my mystery lover. It never occurred to me to look in my own office." He unbuttoned the final button of her blouse, then seductively ran his finger along the edge of her lacy bra.

"I don't know what to say, Mr. Rutledge— Jonathon."

"Say you'll make love with me, right here, right now."

Was this the way it was going to be? She would now be nothing more than his office play toy? It was a possibility Trish hadn't considered. But then she had also admitted to herself that she hadn't thought out the plan very carefully, at least not the part about the consequences should he discover her identity. Nor had she thought out what she wanted after the second night. Would there have been a third and then a fourth night of hot sex and unbridled passion?

Hot sex with Jonathon Rutledge had been

indescribably incredible, but this was so much more. There was a physical connection that throbbed between her legs, but there was an emotional connection that went directly to her heart. Could he possibly be feeling the same thing she was?

She couldn't keep the hint of disappointment out of her voice. "Well, I guess it would be somewhat silly of me to offer any objection at this point."

He cradled her head against his shoulder. "I'm afraid you've misunderstood me. I'm not dictating or assuming. I'm not talking about hot sex or recreational fucking. I'm not expecting you to be at my beck and call whenever I feel the urge. I'm asking if you will make love with me. It has nothing to do with your job or my job, nothing to do with anything in the outside world. It has to do only with you and me—a man and a woman. And then I'd like for us to have dinner tonight, a romantic restaurant at the beach."

Had she heard him correctly? "Dinner at a romantic restaurant?"

"You left me with two very unsettled weekends. I ended up with one pair of red high heels and more thoughts and feelings than I could handle. For three years, we've been working together in a smooth and efficient relationship. I think after what happened the last two Saturday nights, it would be safe to say we also have an incredibly hot physical relationship. So..." He leaned forward and placed a soft kiss on her lips as he caressed her cheek. "I think we should explore what exists between those two extremes, find a solid footing for a lasting relationship."

He brushed another tender kiss against her lips, then offered a hopeful smile. "Will you have dinner with me tonight?"

The biggest risk of her life, what minutes ago had seemed to be a total disaster, had just paid off in the most unexpected way. His smile totally melted her insides and any concerns she still harbored.

"Yes, I'd be honored to have dinner with you." She placed a soft kiss on his lips. "And if that offer to make love is still open, I'd be honored to accept that, too."

"You can consider that a standing offer. Any time and anywhere."

She pointed toward the office door. "Perhaps you'd best lock the door. I don't think this is proper office protocol, and it's definitely against company policy."

He ran his hand seductively across her rear end, locked the door, then gave her his sexiest grin. "I have a feeling there will be lots of things happening in here that won't be proper office protocol...beginning right now."

She returned his smile as she slipped out of her blouse. "I think you're right."

He pulled his shirt off and dropped it on the floor, then kicked off his shoes. "I'm going to reserve the caveman room for after dinner tonight. Now that we don't have to contend with your mask, we can enjoy everything the room has to offer." He cocked his head and stared at her for a moment. "Tell me, my sexy vixen, have you ever made love in a hot tub? Or participated in a quick hot fuck standing up in a waterfall shower?"

"No, I haven't. But I had never done several things before the night of the costume party. It looks like we have a whole new area of excitement we can explore."

Jonathon stopped dead in his tracks, a startled look

on his face followed by a moment of irritation. "Damn…I don't keep any condoms in my office."

The tingle between her legs had turned to a throbbing need. Her pulse raced and her heart pounded. "Then I guess we'll need to make a slight change in our plans."

Words were lost, clothes fell away. The image of the caveman room and what the after dinner hours would bring quickly heated up the mood. Two hungry mouths each with tongues twining together in a seductive ritual. Her hips bucking frantically against his hand as he manipulated her swollen clit. Her hand working his shaft with tantalizing strokes. Neither held back, each pushing for the ecstasy that built to a fever pitch.

She shoved him back onto the couch and climbed on top, her throbbing pussy hovering over his mouth as she wrapped her lips around his pulsing cock. He flicked his tongue against her engorged clit, then sucked it into his mouth. Each of them had been so close to the edge that torrid orgasmic waves came quickly. It took several minutes before their breathing returned to normal.

Jonathon leaned back in the corner of the couch, Trish cradled in his arms. "I hate to disturb this moment, Miss Andrews, but I think we need to get back to work. I have several phone calls to make."

"Of course, Mr. Rutledge. And I have that report to type and distribute to the department managers."

"Well, then…" He flashed a sexy grin. "Until tonight, Miss Andrews? Dinner followed by dessert?"

"Yes." She returned his smile. "Until tonight, Mr. Rutledge."

Steamy Encounter

Chapter One

Afton Pendleton stared out the large oval windows set in the oak double door entrance to the lodge. The last five days had been pure hell and now this—the perfect capper to a miserable week.

The local television newscast referred to the non-stop snowfall that had started night before last as the worst storm in the last fifty years. She slowly shook her head as she emitted a sigh of resignation. Not a thing she could do about it. The local airport closed yesterday afternoon with the snow coming down faster than it could be cleared.

She had busted her butt, making sure everything was in order and ready for the ski resort's grand opening party. As the event planner, a million details had fallen on her shoulders. It was bad enough the resort's owner, Gage Brennan, had made it nearly impossible to do her job from the moment he arrived at the resort. And now it looked as if all her efforts had been for nothing.

The remaining workers had gone home yesterday evening before the snow shut down the entire city. Unlike Afton, most of them were local residents. She had ended up stranded in a luxury ski lodge with Gage Brennan, just the two of them, for who knew how long.

Another ripple of anxiety assaulted her senses. Every verbal exchange with Gage had turned into an argument except for those occasions when she gave in to avoid the inevitable disagreement. And they disagreed about almost everything.

His company had hired her and everything had been running smoothly until five days ago when he arrived in town, unexpected and unannounced. She closed her eyes and visualized the handsome man who had been making her life miserable. He looked to be in his late thirties, much younger than she had assumed— tall, with an athletic build and dark hair. There was no denying his physical appeal and sexual magnetism, in spite of his arrogant attitude.

A tingle of excitement swept through her body, confirming how long it had been since she had sex, at least the *scrape me off the ceiling and fuck me again* type of sex that screamed out for more.

"It doesn't look like it's ever going to stop."

A gasp escaped her throat as she whirled around and found herself staring into the bottomless depths of Gage Brennan's deep blue eyes.

"Oh…Gage. You startled me. I didn't hear you come into the lobby."

"Sorry. I didn't mean to sneak up behind you. It's all this damned snow. It muffles sound, even inside a building." He stared out the window for a moment. "The way things look now it could be days before this stops and people can get around enough for the ski slopes to open."

He flashed what she had come to appreciate as the sexiest smile she had ever seen. In fact, it was that very smile that resulted in her letting him have his way more often than she should have when they disagreed on some facet of the grand opening party. They had been snowed in together since the previous afternoon, and for the entire time she had been fantasizing about him being the one to give her that *scrape me off the ceiling* orgasm she was so in need of. She had even dreamed about it last night.

And for the entire time he had been the perfect gentleman. It was almost as if the circumstances of just the two of them being snowed in at the lodge had put him on his best behavior. He had been overly polite, courteous and so very charming. He had even gone to the lodge's kitchen and prepared dinner for them. Definitely not the same man who had been giving her nothing but grief.

"Well, I guess things could be worse." She tried to put an upbeat sound to her voice. "We have plenty of food and the electricity is still on." She walked across the lobby toward the large fireplace. "And we have lots of firewood in case the power lines go down and we end up without a furnace."

"I've turned the heat way down for most of the lodge. No sense in heating an empty building. The utilities in this part of town are underground, but that doesn't mean the power lines servicing this area couldn't go down. Fortunately, we have generator power as back up. That will be enough to keep the necessities going, such as the kitchen refrigerators and freezers along with the inside emergency lights and outside security lights."

"And there's always those marvelous natural hot springs that feed directly into the pond. Fresh powder on the ski slopes during the day and the hot springs to get the kinks out of the muscles at night. Isn't that what your advertising claims?" The words felt forced, as if she were trying too hard to think of something to say to keep the conversation going.

He crossed the lobby to where she stood in front of the fireplace. "I was just thinking about that. Even though I should take advantage of having all this time to catch up on some paper work, the idea of using the hot springs without anyone else around is very appealing. It was those hot springs that were responsible for me deciding to build this ski resort. It was the one thing that no other resort around here could offer."

Gage moved even closer until their bodies almost touched. He readily admitted that they had certainly engaged in more than their share of disagreements and almost all of them had been instigated by him. There was his vision of how he wanted the grand opening to be, then there was her acknowledged expertise as an event planner. But by no means had all the sparks been irritation, annoyance or anger.

He didn't know about her, but for his part, a lot of those sparks were a lustful desire to be naked in the steamy hot springs with this incredible woman's body rubbing up next to his. Her short red hair and green eyes had immediately captured his attention the moment he met her. She looked to be in her early thirties and didn't wear a wedding ring, not even an engagement ring. That made her available as far as he was concerned.

His plan had been to hit on her after the party when their work relationship had concluded. But also at a time when she was free to leave if she so desired, rather than needing to stay in what she might consider an awkward atmosphere in order to finish her job.

Then the snowstorm hit, and he didn't know what to do. They were stuck together, just the two of them. She had no means of leaving, regardless of how badly she might want to. He felt decidedly uncomfortable with the idea of pressing that kind of an advantage, yet her physical proximity drove him crazy. Last night, alone in his bed in the owner's suite and knowing she was in her room on the second floor, he couldn't think about anything but her.

Just the thought of having his cock buried inside her had resulted in a very hard erection. He wanted to know the taste of her delicious mouth, the texture of her creamy skin and the moist heat of her pussy. But the situation was a tricky line, and he wasn't sure exactly how to navigate, considering their current circumstances.

He placed his fingertips beneath her chin and lifted until they had eye contact. He saw intelligence, curiosity and a sensuality that made his cock twitch and nearly knocked his socks off. He didn't see any anxiety or fear. His intention had been to kiss her, but caution prevailed. "Tell me about yourself. I don't really know anything about you other than you're an event planner and you're from Los Angeles."

The physical contact sent Afton's pulse racing and her heart pounding. The two of them may have been at odds over the grand opening party, but at that moment, she wanted to know him much better, intimately know all of him. Her pussy tingled. The dampness spread to her panties. She wanted that *scrape me off the ceiling* type of hot sex he exuded.

She couldn't stop the slightly husky quality that surrounded her words. "What would you like to know?"

His warm breath whispered across her cheek. "Everything."

For a moment, it seemed as if he had intended to kiss her, but then he apparently changed his mind. Relief or disappointment? She wasn't sure which one she felt.

Granted, the circumstances surrounding them were unusual. They could even be called awkward. But if he was even half as turned on as she was...well, it might be a few days before they could get out or anyone else could get in. A crackling fire in the fireplace, a bottle of champagne, the steamy waters of the hot springs and a building full of bedrooms. Could there be a more perfect set up for seduction?

A more perfect setting for a steamy encounter?

Her words were barely above a whisper. "I'm thirty-three years old, divorced a year ago from a controlling man who didn't think I needed an identity other than being his wife." It took a moment for her to realize exactly what she had said. What she didn't know was *why* she had said it.

"Ah ha...that explains a lot."

Her body stiffened. The sensual blanket covering her had been ripped away in the blink of an eye. She took a quick step backward to put some distance between her and the mesmerizing aura that emanated from him. "And just exactly what is that supposed to mean?"

Once again the sparks of conflict flew between them. "I don't think it *meant* anything. It was merely an observation. You've been resistant to even the slightest suggestion—"

"Suggestion?" The shock of his words jolted

through her. Her anger flared. "You weren't making suggestions. You were demanding impulsive changes to carefully constructed plans based on nothing more than your whim. Days of hard work down the tubes just because you like the color green better than blue—"

His mouth came down hard on hers, not only stilling her words but also driving the thoughts out of her mind. He wrapped her in his embrace, holding her tightly to him. She felt the heat of his passion, an intensity that singed every corner of her reality.

She had been on the receiving end of her share of hot kisses, but nothing like this. It was almost as if her arms had a will of their own as they encircled his neck. She returned his kiss. Her entire being trembled with excitement. Never had anyone so thoroughly grabbed her senses with only a kiss. Her pulse raced. Desire quivered inside her pussy.

The sexiest smile she had ever seen had not been misleading. It belonged to the sexiest man she had ever encountered, a man who had her mind swirling in a cloud of confusion and her body vibrantly alive with both longing and need.

Without warning, he broke off the kiss. He placed his hands on her shoulders and stepped back at arm's length. His gaze almost burned into her as if he were searching for some hidden answer to an even deeper question.

"Before this goes any farther, we need to get something straight." His voice carried a husky quality, and a hint of uncertainty surrounded his words. "We have a very unusual situation here. Neither one of us has the availability of turning around and walking out the door, getting in a car and driving away. We are both confined to this building until the storm lifts enough to get the roads open. The temptation goes without saying."

He paused as if trying to collect his thoughts. "I think I've already made my desires known. But I don't want the circumstances to dictate your actions. I have one very definite rule that I never break. Both people agree and want the same thing or it doesn't happen. And that goes double for now. If you feel in any way that you're being coerced or are uncomfortable all you have to do is say so and that will be the end of it. It's your call."

She tried to collect her thoughts. Until he broke off the kiss, she had been totally mesmerized and ready to go along with anything he wanted. But now that he had given her the opportunity to think, she said the first thought that had come into her mind.

"I admire your directness and appreciate you not trying to press an advantage that could make things very awkward. You're right. This is an extremely unusual situation. Maybe the thing to do is take it a little slower. We've been at odds for five days and you've been behaving like an arrogant ass, but since this storm hit you've been the epitome of politeness and charm. I think I'd like an opportunity to meet the person who must be somewhere between those two extremes."

"That's very level-headed, very logical." He flashed another devastatingly sexy smile. "It wasn't exactly what I wanted to hear, but it's certainly something I can accept. So, when you think you know that person who lives between those extremes well enough, let me know. Until then..." His gaze delved into the depths of her eyes. "Well…I can take no for an answer, but I can't make any promises about being able to stay one hundred percent on my good behavior."

"Fair enough. I've been warned." She had never participated in a more bizarre exchange. On one hand, it was the most honest and straight forward conversation about having sex she had ever been involved in. But on the other hand, it almost seemed impersonal, too matter-of-fact. Mechanical rather than physical or emotional. She believed what he told her, if she said no, he would respect it. She also knew her pussy throbbed from the all-too-brief kiss that curled her toes and generated enough heat to melt the snow outside the door.

But what about Gage Brennan? Was this type of *spontaneous* behavior nothing more than business as usual for him? Was it something that didn't mean any more than a hot fuck in the back seat of a car or a one night stand? She had been away from the dating scene for seven years—six years of marriage followed by one year of sexless divorce.

Truth be known, she just hadn't met anyone since her divorce who grabbed her attention. No one had made her cream her panties. No one had made her pulse race. No one had kissed her with a heated passion that flowed through her entire body setting off sparks of wanton desire.

No one…until now.

She tried to settle the nervousness jittering inside her but without much success. She cleared her throat. "So…tell me about yourself."

He stepped in closer, until their bodies were almost touching again. "What would you like to know?"

"Everything." Her breathless reply told her just how much of an impact this sexy man had on her.

"I'm thirty-nine years old." His words tickled across her cheek. "My wife and I have been legally separated for three years and would have been divorced two years and eleven months ago if we could have agreed on a settlement."

Gage touched her hair and breathed in the spicy fragrance of her perfume. "I don't think this hands off thing is going to work." His words sounded raspy, even to his own ear.

"I don't think so, either." Her words were barely audible.

His mouth came down on hers, infusing her with all the passion coursing through his body. He tasted her sweetness, a treat that whetted his appetite for more…a lot more. He wanted it all. The feel of his cock buried deep inside her. The burning intensity of her pussy muscles kneading his hard shaft as he shuttled in and out. The sensation of her lips wrapped around his hardness. The heat radiating from her pussy to his face as he sucked on her clit. He wanted to know every inch of her body, then he wanted to get to know it all over again.

For the last few days just being in the same room with her had nearly driven him to distraction. It had a lot to do with the testy attitude he displayed toward her. It was more a defense mechanism to protect his vulnerability than anything else. But the time for defensiveness was over.

No doubt about it. The hands off agreement was history. He tangled his fingers in the silky strands of her hair. He had never met a woman who so immediately set his libido on fire and made his cock twitch. He tentatively probed between her lips with his tongue.

After a moment's hesitation, she opened her mouth to accept the intrusion. He twined his tongue with hers, thrusting it into her mouth the same way he wanted to thrust his cock into her pussy. He pulled her tighter against him. Even with the barrier of heavy winter clothing, the feel of her breasts pressed against his chest as they rose and fell with her ragged breathing excited his need and fed his hunger. On more than one occasion, he had fantasized about her naked body writhing beneath him in orgasmic rapture. Was his fantasy about to become reality?

His arousal had grown to full erection. He ran his hand down her back, then up underneath her sweatshirt. He slid his hand across her bare skin, confirming what he already knew—she wasn't wearing a bra. He moved his hand around her rib cage until he was able to fondle the fullness of her breast and tease her puckered nipple. A throaty moan of pleasure filled the air, but he wasn't sure whether it had come from her or from him. Perhaps both of them.

He pulled his mouth away from hers. Her slightly parted, kiss-swollen lips tugged at every lustful thought that had ever gone through his mind. He took a calming breath in an attempt to restore his equilibrium. She had been too close, too tempting. He hadn't been able to resist the urge to kiss her, but he had not been prepared for the impact it had on the few remaining threads of his self-control.

"Let's move this to my suite unless you want to fuck right here and now on the lobby floor." His words came out as a breathless rasp.

A ringing sound came from his pocket, the cell phone demanding his attention. "Damn!" He pulled his hand from her breast as he momentarily rested his cheek against the top of her head. "Fucking damn phone." He pulled it from his pocket, checked the caller ID, then flipped it open.

"Brennan."

"I have a new update from the divorce front. Once again, money is the central theme."

He listened intently, clenching his jaw in anger as his attorney gave him the bad news. "Not a chance. Tell her and that shyster bastard she calls an attorney that hell will freeze over before I give her control of any of my companies. I came home and found my wife in my bed fucking her brains out with not just one man, but two. No way am I going to pay her for that. I made her a generous offer. In fact, it was more than generous, all things considered. That's all there is. There won't be any more." He glanced out the window. Perhaps he should have worded that differently. From the look of things hell could possibly be in the process of freezing as he spoke.

As Gage continued his phone conversation, Afton managed to slip out of his embrace. She put some physical distance between her and this very disconcerting man who made her pulse race and her heart pound with excitement. What she had heard definitely touched a sympathetic spot inside her.

So, they each had baggage and issues left over from a bad marriage. She had an overbearing and controlling husband and he had a cheating wife. Did that give them something in common? Some sort of neutral ground where they could build something new?

She shook her head. What the hell was she thinking? He was a very sexy man whose kisses curled her toes. That was all there was to it. An intense physical attraction that made her neglected pussy pulse with need. And the feel of his erection as it pressed against her hip told her he was certainly equipped to satisfy that need.

An abstract thought invaded her mind, one that seemed to gain momentum with each passing second. A very short-lived affair with a sexy man she barely knew while trapped at a ski lodge in a snowstorm. A no-strings-attached sexathon. Something to satisfy that itch between her legs.

Did she dare engage in such outrageous behavior? Being promiscuous was not her style. If she was the type who hopped into the sack with every man who crossed her path, she wouldn't have the itch that was in bad need of being satisfied. Once the roads were cleared they would go their separate ways—a steamy encounter would satisfy all her pent up sexual tension and frustrations but wouldn't interfere with her life or her career.

She glanced toward Gage who was still involved with his phone call. She wandered toward the French doors that led from the lobby to the enclosed swimming pool and the adjacent pond fed from the hot springs. At the far end of the stone lined pond was a small waterfall cascading over natural rock. The springs maintained a constant year round temperature of one hundred three degrees. Beyond that, the large expanses of glass gave a breathtaking view of the mountains and the forest. And at that moment, a view of the overabundance of snow.

She took off her shoes and socks, rolled the legs of

her sweatpants up to her knees and sat on one of the boulders edging the pond. She dangled her legs in the water, the gentle swirl completely different from the intensity of the large spa with all of its air jets.

"Let's see…where were we before that phone call so rudely interrupted us?"

His voice startled her. She didn't know how long she had been sitting there, lost in thought. She quickly looked around and saw him standing behind her. "You're very good at that, walking up behind someone without making any noise."

"Quite the contrary. You were so engrossed in your own thoughts you failed to hear me." He kneeled down next to her, cocked his head and shot a curious look in her direction. "What had your attention so focused?"

Afton sat there like a bump on a log, staring into his eyes without answering his question. She wanted to say something but couldn't force out any words. Once again the mesmerizing pull of his blue eyes grabbed hold of her and refused to let go.

At that moment, whatever he wanted she would gladly have given and that most definitely included having their naked bodies tangled together in hot passion. Her pulse quickened at the thought. Another rush of moisture soaked her panties. That nagging itch became so insistent that she had difficulty sitting still. Her pussy cried out for attention even if it was only from her vibrator, but her vibrator was definitely not her first choice.

He leaned his face very close to hers. "Oh…I guess you were thinking about a personal matter that you don't want to talk about."

Before she could respond, he captured her mouth

again with a searing intensity that sent sparks shooting through her body. She wanted his cock inside her and she wanted it now. Her hands went to his chest. She felt the hard-muscled planes through the soft cashmere of his sweater. He surely had to be the sexiest man alive. The very air surrounding them crackled with sexual energy. Her pussy throbbed. She shifted her weight so she could rub her clit against the boulder she was sitting on in an attempt to scratch a little bit of that sexual craving.

It was as if he had read her mind and noticed the way she squirmed. "Let me help you with that." His husky words matched her ragged breathing. He worked his hand inside the elastic waistband of her sweatpants. He scraped his fingers across her muff, then dipped a fingertip between her pussy lips into the moist heat. A sharp jolt ricocheted through her body. He shoved his finger all the way inside her as he thrust his tongue into her mouth.

The combination set her on fire. She both heard and felt the moan of pleasure leave her throat. An involuntary pelvic thrust shoved her pussy against his hand. She reached for his crotch and found his erection straining against the front of his jeans. He was as hard as she was wet. She rubbed the outside of his jeans, then lowered the zipper and wiggled her hand inside until she could cradle his balls through the cotton fabric of his briefs. His sensual groan filled her mouth. He added a second finger in her pussy while stimulating her clit with his thumb.

The delicious waves of excitement swirled around inside her. She couldn't have stayed still even if her life depended on it. She thrust her pussy against his hand with the same rhythm he had set with his fingers. It had been much too long since she had an orgasm that didn't involve her vibrator. His attentions pushed her closer and closer to the edge much faster than she wanted. Then it began—the contractions inside her pussy, the convulsions deep inside her body.

The delicious waves of ecstasy. She threw her head back, momentarily breaking off the kiss.

Gage had never seen a face more exquisite or more desirable while in the throes of orgasm. Her eyelids fluttered shut. A flush of sexual excitement spread across her cheeks. Her chest heaved as she gulped in each breath. The sight of her parted lips, wet and kiss-swollen, sent an additional surge through his cock. He hadn't been prepared for her to climax so quickly. Moving his fingers through her folds, he spread her juices along the edges of her pussy lips and over her sensitive clit while trying to bring his labored breathing under control.

She slowly opened her eyes. The fires of passion burned in their emerald depths. It upped his level of arousal by several degrees. She withdrew her hand from inside his jeans, instilling a sudden sense of loss. His hard cock throbbed, begging for more attention.

He had been vaguely aware of how precariously she was perched on the edge of the boulder. The reality hit him full force when she lost her balance. He tried to jerk his hand from inside her sweatpants but ended up tangled in her panties instead. A moment of panic hit as she grabbed his arm in an attempt to keep from falling. His valiant attempt to hold on to her came too late. They tumbled into the pond, hitting the water with a loud splash that echoed off the glass walls.

After several tries, he managed to free his hand from its entanglement. They struggled to find their footing on the bottom on the pond, finally regaining their balance in the waist deep water of the natural hot springs. Gazes locked together for several seconds, neither sure of what to do. The ambiance changed swiftly from shock to realization and confusion, culminating in laughter.

"I was about to say that was a quick way to dampen the mood, but decided against it." He smoothed her wet hair away from her face and noted the way her wet sweatshirt clung to the curve of her breasts.

Afton returned his teasing grin. "Yes, I believe *dampen* is the operative word."

His manner turned serious. "Perhaps we should get out of these wet clothes..." A shortness of breath grabbed at him. He tried to get his thoughts straight, but it was no use. Pulling her body to him, he brought his mouth down on hers. His tongue invaded the intimate recesses. She opened her mouth to his overture and wrapped her arms around his neck. Her immediate response fueled his already heated desires.

After what seemed like several minutes, he finally broke off the delicious kiss. "We either get out of this pond and go to my suite, or we get out of our clothes and toss them on the surrounding rocks. Now that we've sampled the appetizer, I think it's time we moved on to the main course."

"It would be foolish of me to object at this point after we've just—"

He froze for a second, then quickly but reluctantly turned loose of her. Her words hit him hard and left him uncertain. "Do you have objections? If so, now would be the time to say so."

A bit of a shy smile turned the corners of her mouth. "No...no objections."

Gage climbed up the stone steps, then extended his hand to help Afton out of the pond. Water dripped from their clothes, creating a large puddle around their feet. He pulled his cell phone from his pocket. "I suppose I need to get this thing dried out and see if it still works."

She removed her watch from her wrist. "Same here." She gestured toward his sweater. "This water probably hasn't done that cashmere much good, either."

The spontaneous moment of heated desire had been broken. More practical matters pushed to the forefront. He grabbed a couple of large towels from the cupboard against the wall and handed one to her. He wiped off his cell phone, towel dried his hair, then slung the towel around the back of his neck. He watched as she dried the excess water from her hair. When she finished, he placed his fingertips under her chin and lifted until he could look into her eyes. He brushed a soft kiss across her lips. "This isn't exactly what I had in mind."

An awkward moment of silence followed, then he continued. "I know you've been just about everywhere in the lodge, but let me show you some place you haven't been. Let me show you my suite."

Without saying another word, he took her hand. She left her shoes and socks on the floor next to the pond. He led her through the lobby, behind the registration area and down a hallway to a door with a sign that read *PRIVATE—Do Not Enter*. On the other side of the door was a private elevator, a staircase and a door leading outside. They took the elevator to the top floor and emerged on a landing that also included the stairs from the ground floor. He opened the door to the penthouse suite, then stepped aside so she could enter.

She knew the penthouse suite existed, but it had not been part of her plans for the grand opening party. She stopped in stunned silence as she looked around the room. It was a completely different look and feel from the décor of the lodge. This reflected the taste of the man who owned it. This was his private sanctuary and it was magnificent.

Large expanses of glass took advantage of the incredible views. A stone fireplace dominated the room. Different portions of the room were clearly defined by use, but everything was open with one area flowing into another. It was made for entertaining. They walked up the curved staircase to the loft, which overlooked the expanse below. It contained a private seating alcove away from the main floor of the suite along with a small area designated as an office.

Her gaze slowly traveled across the scene below her and then took in the loft. She turned toward him. "This is beautiful. You can really get away from the hustle and bustle of the lodge in here, just as if you were miles away in an isolated mountain cabin…albeit, a luxurious mountain cabin. You can have complete privacy."

"That was my intention. A place where I could get away and truly relax. I even have my own private ski lift to the top of the slope." He pulled her body against him, holding her in his embrace. "Do you snow ski?"

"A little. I'm not very good. I think I probably spend more time on my butt than I do on the skis. Unfortunately, I've never had enough time to really practice so that I could get any better. My work schedule keeps me pretty busy."

"Maybe you can make some time when this storm clears and the slopes open." His words became soft, his voice conveying an intimate feeling.

"I do have a couple of free days, providing the weather clears soon." She had trouble forcing out the words. She was more than aware of his erection pressing against her and the way he sensually ran his hands across her shoulders, down her back, then caressed her rear end. It was almost as if there were two layers of reality unfolding at the same time, the surface layer of polite chit chat and the underlying current of sexual tension and heated desire. Her pulse quickened and her breathing grew ragged. Surely, he could feel her heart pounding. The quick orgasm he provided her with his fingers had only told her she wanted much more of Gage Brennan.

"Let me show you the rest of my suite. I'll build a fire in the fireplace. I don't want you to chill and end up with a cold or the flu because of your wet clothes."

He opened the double doors and stepped aside so she could enter the master suite. Again, the glass walls brought the outside into the room. She could tell by looking that it was one way glass. Occupants of the room could see out, but people outside could not see in, even when the bedroom lights were turned on, which made it perfect. There was total privacy without shutting out the magnificence of all outdoors whether day or night.

"Now, if I recall correctly," he pulled her into his arms, ran his hand under her sweatshirt and cupped the fullness of her breast, "we were about like this when my phone rang."

Her entire body quivered with excitement. "What if it rings again?"

"I don't even know if it still works. But just as a precaution, I turned if off. The answering machine will answer the lodge's phone. There's nothing and no one to bother us."

Then his mouth claimed hers with a heated kiss, putting a stop to any further conversation. She willingly accepted his tongue, the texture meshing with hers in a seductive twining. Her breathing grew labored as her ardor increased. She felt an immediate sense of loss when he removed his hand from her breast, a loss he dispelled when he pulled her sweatshirt up until her breasts were exposed. Bending forward, he took one of her nipples into his mouth. His gentle suckling evoked a soft moan from her.

His raspy words floated into her consciousness. "We need to get you out of those wet clothes."

Her own words were equally breathless. "The same can be said for you, too."

Nothing else needed to be said. They each peeled off their wet clothes. A hard surge of lust jolted through her as she raked his gaze over his nude form. His cock stood hard in full erection, obviously ready and from all appearances very capable of delivering. Her pussy tingled in anticipation.

She watched as he built a fire in the fireplace. A moment later he had his arms wrapped around her body and his lips wrapped around her tautly puckered nipple.

Chapter Two

Even Gage's strong embrace was not enough to prevent Afton from falling backward when her calves bumped against the bed. But it was not enough to dislodge his mouth from her breast. He had a suction hold on her nipple. The sensation sent a rush of heated desire rippling through her body. She ran her hands across the hard planes of his chest, then down to his muscular thighs. She brushed her hand along the length of his shaft. His groan of pleasure triggered a soft moan from her. She craved the sensation of his bare skin along the length of her naked torso.

Never had she seen a more perfect specimen of the male physique than Gage Brennan, right down to and definitely including the most beautiful penis—perfect in shape, definition and size. The ultimate sex toy that could give any woman untold hours of pleasure. And from the look of things, he had enough stamina to provide all that and more. Just the sight of his hard cock made her mouth water, not to mention what it was doing to her very wet pussy.

Gage allowed her nipple to slip from his mouth as he pulled back to look at her. He had never wanted a woman more than he wanted her. The heated passion glowing in the depths of her eyes told him just how incredible sex with Afton Pendleton was going to be. She had the most perfect breasts he had ever seen. And his all too brief physical encounter with them confirmed they were real rather than a purchased boob job. Her full firm breasts were capped by delicious looking nipples just begging to be nibbled and sucked. A barely contained excitement coursed through his body. The memory of the way her pussy closed in around his finger when they were at the hot springs pond and her heated response to his touch remained vivid in his mind.

Kneeling on the bed next to her, he teased her nipples with his tongue then kissed his way down her body. His nostrils flared as he inhaled the intoxicating aroma of her heated sex. The auburn curls adorning her mound said her boobs weren't the only thing about her that was real. She was also a natural redhead. With her physical attributes being genuine, there was a good chance everything about her was real...her attitudes, desires, responses. Everything.

She spread her legs in invitation, and he liked what he saw. If she was even half as hot and a fourth as horny as he was, they were in for an afternoon of the greatest sex imaginable. Two people thrown together in an isolated setting—time had no meaning. They could fuck themselves into oblivion, then start all over again. Her quick pelvic thrust invited him to bury his mouth in her muff. And he happily obliged.

He scooped his arms under her legs and lifted them over his shoulders, opening her entire pussy to him. He snaked his tongue along the outer edges of her slit, flicking and teasing her pussy lips as he circled the opening. Her taste filled his mouth, the spicing as intoxicating as her scent. A gasp escaped her throat as her body stiffened when he laved her erect clit with the flat of his tongue. Her hips jerked upward, shoving her pussy hard against his mouth. He wiggled his tongue as far into the well as it would reach, scoured her tunnel walls, then withdrew.

He felt her entire body quiver as he did it again and again, each time also stimulating her engorged clit. Her pussy walls tried to grab and hold his tongue. Her moans of pleasure matched the way she continued to rub her clit against his mouth with ever increasing fervor. His cock throbbed with need, but he didn't want to give up the marvelous feast laid out in front of him. Every moan, every tremor of her body fed his all-consuming desire for her. A desire that had turned into a deep physical need. But was it a need for more than hot sex with a beautiful woman?

Her kiss, her breasts, her taste, her scent, the texture of her pussy lips and clit—there had never been a more perfect match between what she offered and what excited him. Simply put, she was the most exquisite woman he had ever been with and his cock hadn't even gotten near her pussy yet.

Afton cried out as the orgasmic waves convulsed through her.

His lips closed around her pulsing clit, the sucking motion increasing the already intense sensations of her release. Her hips bucked wildly, an involuntary action totally out of her control. New waves of rapture surged through her body. She ran her fingers through his hair as she held his head tightly against her pussy. The fervor deepened, the euphoria heightened. Any grasp she might have had on reality spiraled into oblivion.

It seemed like forever before he finally released his suction hold on her engorged clit and lifted his face from between her thighs. Forever before she finally came down from her orgasmic high. Her chest heaved as she tried to catch her breath. Her pussy convulsed to the point where it almost vibrated from the overwhelming pleasure his mouth had given her. At that moment, it was difficult for her to believe this was the same man who had been a major source of irritation and annoyance in her life for nearly a week.

"Holy shit! That's incredible." Her words shot out in a breathless rush, then trailed off into a deep sensual moan oozing the pure sexual abandon that filled every corner of her reality.

The sound reverberated through Gage's body and tugged at every fiber of his existence. His cock ached for the hot nest located between her sleek thighs, his throbbing need screamed for release.

He grabbed the condom packet from the drawer in the night stand and ripped it open. As he started to roll it on, her hand stilled his efforts. She quickly rolled it on for him, then cradled his balls in her hand. Her touch nearly sent him over the edge. He suspected he was about to participate in the ultimate fuck to die for. Something so special it overshadowed any and all past encounters.

His arms trembled as he supported his weight above her, his cock head poised at the entrance of her pussy. He slowly pushed forward, a tantalizing inch by inch until he had his length fully embedded inside her. Her pussy walls closed around his shaft, encasing him in a tight sheath of hot wet velvet. He had never experienced anything like it. A low growl of primal lust clawed its way out of his throat. He remained propped up on his elbows so he could watch her face.

Her eyes fluttered shut as her tongue darted out from between slightly parted lips. He attempted to set a slow pace as he stroked in and out, but his pent up need became too much. He pumped faster, each of his down strokes met with an equally enthusiastic upward thrust of her hips. She wrapped her legs around his waist, shoving her heels against his ass to add emphasis to each of his forward thrusts. He rammed his cock inside her to the hilt with each deep plunge. He wanted to give her yet another orgasm before he totally lost it.

The glow that covered her face during orgasm excited him more than he thought possible. Her breasts bounced and jiggled as she writhed beneath him. His balls churned as he rushed toward his own release. He was only seconds away when her legs tightened around his body. She shoved her pussy hard against him and ground her clit into his pubic bone.

The sound of her loud moan and feel of her orgasmic contractions sent him over the edge. Hard spasms shuddered through his body as his semen spurted into the condom. His arms quivered with the intensity of his release, causing him to fall on top of her. He buried his face in her hair and held her tightly as they each joined in the power of the shared orgasm.

No other woman had ever made him feel the depths of what he had just experienced with Afton. It confirmed his earlier thought that every sexual encounter from his past had been nothing more than routine fucking. Just a preliminary round in preparation for the main event. He placed a series of tender kisses across her forehead and cheeks while fighting to regain his breath.

"You are so fucking incredible. I have never

experienced anything like you. You have the most exquisite pussy—" The expression on her face froze the rest of his thought in his throat before it could become even more damaging words. It had all come out totally wrong.

"I'm sorry…I didn't mean that the way it sounded." There wasn't any way that he considered her as nothing more than a pussy, some place to bury his cock and shoot his load. She was intelligent, beautiful, warm, and so very responsive. And she had an independence he found very appealing in spite of her obvious opinion of him to the contrary.

She was just the type of woman who could make him change his mind about relationships if he wasn't careful.

She excited him so much that even his powerful orgasm hadn't been enough to curtail his highly aroused condition. A partial erection remained and was already beginning to harden to its full extension again.

The sensation of his cock growing harder and longer while still inside her sent a ripple of desire coursing through Afton. What a moment ago had been the afterglow of the most incredible series of orgasms she had ever experienced was now the escalating excitement of renewal that had her body pulsing with need. His hard shaft once again filled her. She did a couple of small pelvic thrusts that allowed her to grind her clit against him again. It did something else, too. It said he needed to dispose of the used condom that still sheathed his cock. She could tell from the expression on his face it told him the same thing.

He carefully withdrew, then slid out of bed. He leaned over her and brushed a quick kiss across her mouth. "Don't go anywhere. Don't you dare move. I'll be right back."

She allowed a teasing grin as she gestured toward the window and the heavy snowfall. "Where would I go?" She watched as he hurried toward the bathroom.

His words about not having meant what he said floated through her mind. She hadn't taken any offense, especially since she had a similar type of thought about him. The most fabulous cock she had ever known. But that didn't mean it was her only interest in him. He had many more qualities she wanted to know.

She closed her eyes and visualized the incredible Gage Brennan. She could be content spending the rest of her life with their bodies tangled together in hot wild sex.

She shoved that thought away with a frown. It was certainly the most impractical notion that had ever invaded her mind. Well, maybe not the *most* impractical. Her decision to spend the time they were confined to the lodge in no-strings-attached hot sex had been as far removed from practical as possible.

As much as this man sent her spiraling to the far reaches of ecstasy, she was her own person. She enjoyed her work. She would never be just *the little woman* or someone who had no identity other than some rich man's sexual play toy.

Then the euphoria invaded her mind again. It had been one hell of an afternoon of sex, one she'd never forget. And it wasn't over yet. She may have forgotten her first kiss, remembered that her first sexual experience had been very disappointing and not much else about it, but she would never forget the last few hours. If there was ever a *scrape me off the ceiling and fuck me again* orgasm, Gage Brennan had been responsible for it. And again was what she wanted. Again and again. She strongly suspected she would never have her fill of him. She also suspected something else. He had ruined her chances of ever achieving total sexual contentment with any other man.

Her thoughts were interrupted when she felt his weight press into the bed. The sight of his half hard cock pleased her, but she wanted him fully erect and as physically ready as the glow in his eyes said he was. She took the initiative, being more aggressive than she normally would—more aggressive than she had ever been with any man. But, the circumstances were far from normal.

She placed little kisses and nips across his chest and down his belly until arriving at his rapidly growing cock. She laved her tongue across the smooth head as she wrapped her hand around his girth. His groan of submission excited her almost as much as the sensation of his tautly drawn skin and engorged veins beneath her fingers.

He quickly rolled on a new condom, nudged his knee between her legs to open them wider, then settled his body over hers. His length filled her as it had before. Her heart pounded in her chest and her breath came in hard gasps. No one else's cock had ever felt so good inside her, had ever promised and delivered such earth shattering, mind blowing orgasms. The kind of torrid sex most people only dreamed about but never experienced. Then his mouth came down on hers and all thoughts came to an abrupt halt.

His rhythm was smooth and sure. She met each of his down strokes with an upward thrust of her hips.

They moved in unison, a harmonious coupling so perfectly attuned that it was as if they had been long time lovers. His pace increased, his momentum coming harder and faster. His tongue meshed with hers, twining in a ritual that increased the level of excitement surging through her body. Layer after layer of intensity built inside her. The contractions convulsed in waves that swept through her entire reality, engulfing her in the ultimate euphoria. She wrapped her arms and legs tightly around his body and held on.

Gage drove one last deep plunge inside her. He held on to her as tightly as she held him. Wrapped in each other's arms, his cock buried to the hilt inside her pussy, they each allowed the incendiary rapture to flow through them.

The fire crackled in the fireplace, the woodsy scent of burning pine wafting through the air. The heavy, wet snow continued to shroud everything in a deep blanket of white. Time seemed to stand still for several minutes as they remained with their bodies entwined, savoring the emotional as well as physical delights of their shared orgasm. He finally raised his head, brushed her hair away from the damp skin of her face, then placed a soft kiss on her lips. He held her tightly. Neither one of them wanted to let go.

****

Gage stood just inside the bedroom door. He watched Afton as she warmed herself in front of the fire. He had given her his pajama top to wear until she could get some dry clothes from her room on the second floor of the lodge. She glanced out the window at the snow, then returned her attention to the fireplace. He wasn't sure exactly what to make of the expression that clouded her features. Could it be regret?

He shook his head in confusion, touched by a bit of apprehension. No doubt in his mind that it had been the best sex he ever experienced. But did she regret her decision to engage in incredibly hot sex with him? A slight frown wrinkled across his forehead. Or could she be regretting that she had allowed him to coerce her? He didn't like that thought, and he didn't like the implications.

He wanted to know so much more of her. He would be a happy camper if they stayed in his bed until the storm passed. Could that possibly be her concern? Did she feel trapped? Had she reluctantly consented and now she wondered how much more he would want? And how often? It was a consideration that continued to play through his mind as he walked across the room. It left him uneasy and concerned about what to do and how to proceed.

"Here." Gage held out the shoes and socks toward Afton. "I retrieved these from next to the pond."

She whirled around, surprise covering her face. "You did it again, walked up behind me without making any noise."

He gestured toward the floor and flashed what he hoped was a casual smile. "Thick carpeting."

She took the shoes and socks from him, then set them on the floor next to the loveseat. "Thank you. I just checked my clothes. They're still damp."

"I can take them down to the laundry facility and put them in the dryer if you'd like." He hesitated a moment, not sure of what else to say. "Or...I could go to your room and get some dry clothes for you."

He carefully watched her reaction to his words. He

hadn't been sure about making that offer. Would it sound as if he expected her to continue to stay in his suite? It had been a long time since he had been so unsure of himself, least of all with a woman.

She offered what seemed to him to be an almost shy smile. "There isn't anyone else in the building to see me. I could certainly return to my room dressed like this and put on clean, dry clothes."

It wasn't what he wanted to hear. "You had a very pensive look on your face when I walked in. Is something wrong?" He drew in a calming breath, then ventured the question that was really on his mind. "Are you having regrets?" He knew the anxiety came through in his voice, but he wasn't able to prevent it. And from the look on her face he knew she had noticed it, too.

"No...no regrets." Her voice softened, conveying an emotional moment of vulnerability. "I guess I was just a little overwhelmed. This isn't at all what I had anticipated when I woke up this morning."

A wave of relief swept through him. He wanted to pull her into his arms but suddenly felt awkward about it...unsure of himself. How strange. What was there about this woman? He had never been unsure of himself where women were concerned, but he could not deny the uncertainty coursing through his veins. "I have to admit that I'm also a little surprised by everything that's happened."

He quickly changed gears, not wanting to make her think that sex was the only thing on his mind. "I'm hungry. How about you? I have a few things in the refrigerator here. If there isn't anything that grabs your interest, we can check the lodge's kitchen. I know for a fact that the freezers are filled in anticipation of the grand opening this weekend. Unfortunately, so are the refrigerators. Most of that will probably need to be thrown out. Definitely an unexpected expense."

"I was thinking about that, too. It's going to be such a waste. I imagine there's a lot of it that will still be good for several days yet, but according to health codes you won't be able to serve it in the restaurant. If this weather clears enough for people to be able to get out tomorrow maybe you can find a place to donate it, maybe a shelter of some sort."

"That's a good idea. But for now...let's see what we can find for ourselves."

"Yes, I'm hungry."

Chapter Three

Afton and Gage sat at the breakfast bar in the kitchenette of his suite. They had raided the lodge refrigerator and gathered a variety of fresh vegetables and fruits and a couple of steaks to take back to his suite. It wasn't long before they were enjoying a delicious meal, food Gage prepared while Afton watched rather than him simply assuming she would do the cooking.

When they had finished eating, he poured some more wine into her glass. "Would you like anything else? We haven't tackled the freezer yet. I know there's ice cream and undoubtedly several other dessert items."

"No, thank you. I've had plenty." It wasn't a hunger for food that whetted her appetite. There was a churning deep inside her, a hunger for more of Gage Brennan. A whole lot more. "Tasty and it hit the spot. You're a good cook."

"I live alone and sometimes get tired of eating microwave meals so I learned to do some cooking out of necessity."

"I assumed you would eat most of your meals out."

He cocked his head and leveled a questioning gaze in her direction. "You mean life in the fast lane where I'm never home? Out at a different club every night?"

"Something like that." The crimson heat flushed across her cheeks. Her sheepish response was certainly inadequate, but she hadn't known what else to say.

"Well, I'm sorry to shatter your illusion, but that's not my lifestyle."

She didn't know how to reply to his statement. He had not said it in anger or even disapproval, but it did put her on notice about making assumptions concerning his personal life. It was an awkward moment. In order to break the tension, she gathered up their dishes and carried them to the sink.

"Don't worry about those. Housekeeping will—"

An amused chuckle escaped her throat. "I don't think so. At least not right away. First, someone working in housekeeping has to be able to get through this storm to come to work."

A hint of embarrassment flashed across his face as he glanced away in an obvious attempt to cover it. "Right...there is no housekeeping."

The quick glimpse into his vulnerability touched a warm spot inside her. It was an endearing quality she never would have associated with him. Each little nuance of the real Gage Brennan that slipped through into the open allowed her yet another insight into the real man rather than the projected image he chose to present to others. She was beginning to know the man that lived between the extremes. And she liked him. She liked him very much.

It went beyond the earth-moving orgasms. She knew she would still like him even if they never made love again. A little shiver told her that the idea of never being hot and naked with Gage Brennan again would be a true disaster in every sense of the word. But that didn't stop the realization that she wanted more with him than merely *scrape me off the ceiling and fuck me again* sex. But how much more?

She watched as he cleared the rest of the items from the breakfast bar, then loaded the dishwasher. Everything about him excited her. She studied his smooth, fluid motions, the way his body moved as he bent and stretched. He had pulled on the pajama bottoms that matched the top he had given her to wear. The bare well-defined planes of his hard chest and his broad shoulders were like the tip of the iceberg. His long muscular legs, tight ass and incredible penis were hidden from view.

She wandered over to the large wall of glass and gazed out at the snow. Her mind drifted over the last few hours, over the incredibly hot sex that had driven her to the heights of euphoria, far beyond any place she had ever been with any other man. As she continued to stare at the trees and mountains, the realization slowly seeped into her consciousness.

It had almost stopped snowing. At least, it was not coming down in blizzard torrents as it had been. Had the storm finally spent its fury and was about to move on? It wouldn't be long before the road crews would be clearing away the snow so that people could once again get out and go about their business.

A tremor of apprehension confirmed what she knew. It also meant it wouldn't be much longer before some of the employees returned to the lodge, possibly as early as first thing in the morning. And that would put an end to their interlude. She gathered her determination. If this was going to be her last opportunity to experience the most incredible sex of her life, then she wanted to take full advantage of it.

A strong arm slipped around her waist, and warm

breath tickled across the side of her neck, startling her out of her thoughts.

"It looks like the snow has almost stopped." His sexy voice fed her desires. "It will be dark in less than half an hour, but I bet we'll have blue sky and sunshine in the morning."

She placed her arm on top of his and leaned against his chest. "I was just thinking the same thing. By tomorrow morning, people will be coming out of hiding and things will start returning to normal."

An audible sigh of resignation escaped his throat. "Yes, back to *normal*. Back to a ton of work in rescheduling the grand opening party. Back to the stress and pressure of daily business."

She turned and gave him a curious look. "You sound like you'd rather not bother with any of it."

Gage held her in his embrace, turning her words over in his mind. He felt more comfortable around Afton than he ever had around anyone else. And that very sense of comfort was beginning to concern him. The sex was the hottest he had ever engaged in and he genuinely liked her, but he was beginning to think they might have more.

He took a steadying breath in an attempt to calm the sudden wave of nervousness that washed through him. "I'll tell you something I've never told anyone before." He brushed a soft kiss across her lips, then cradled her head against his shoulder. His heartfelt words came out as a near whisper. "Sometimes I do get tired of it. There have been occasions when I wanted to walk out of a board of directors meeting, catch a flight to some exotic place where no one knew me and leave all the headaches to someone else."

"I hadn't thought of that before, of the pressure and stress someone in your position would carry on your shoulders. I guess I had bought into the concept that anyone who had a lot of money was leading a life of pleasure, a lifestyle everyone else would envy."

"Don't get me wrong, I like the things the money provides. I also like the opportunities afforded to me because of it. But it's not the same thing as being footloose and fancy free. I could turn my back on everything right now, walk away and be very comfortable financially for the rest of my life without needing to do another day's work. But I have a lot of people depending on me for their livelihood. There's a lot of pressure in that type of responsibility and I take my responsibilities very seriously."

He smoothed a loose tendril of her hair away from her cheek as he delved into the depth of her eyes. "I've enjoyed this interlude that the storm brought. No telephones ringing, not being pulled in five different directions at the same time, no one demanding immediate decisions to problems that don't have any ready solutions." He placed a soft kiss on her lips. "And most of all I've enjoyed being here with you. I've never had a more pleasant surprise than what today has brought into my life."

Her gaze dropped to the floor as the pink tinge spread across her cheeks and forehead and her voice quieted to an emotion laden whisper. "Thank you." She regained eye contact with him. "This has been quite a surprise for me, too."

He arched a questioning eyebrow. "A pleasant one, I hope."

A tender smile turned the corners of her mouth.

"Yes, a very pleasant one."

He emitted a sigh of contentment as he continued to hold her in his arms. "You know what?"

"No, what?"

He pressed his lips to her forehead. "You're too comfortable to be around. You bring out my hidden thoughts and feelings and that's bad."

"Why is it bad?"

"Because it takes away my advantage."

"I didn't realize we were negotiating a business deal."

He tilted his head back so that he could see her face. "We're not. This isn't business. It's personal. But what I don't know is exactly what—" His mind shut off the words before he could complete the thought. Yes, indeed...she was much too comfortable and he was growing more confused and uncertain by the minute.

He shifted gears into the smooth, practiced outer persona he hid behind in his dealings with everyone. He glanced out the window again. "It looks like only a few isolated flakes falling. The road crews are probably already digging out so they can start clearing the roads. I think we should make the most of the time while we still have the entire lodge to ourselves."

He nuzzled her neck, then kissed her cheek. "What would you say to some skinny dipping in the pool? Or if you prefer warmer water, we could cavort in the spring fed pond."

"I think that sounds like a terrific idea."

****

Afton packed an overnight bag while Gage waited at the door to her room. There hadn't been any conversation, discussion or even a question. After a steamy interlude in the spring fed pond, they went to her room in the lodge so she could grab a few things before spending the night in his suite. She closed her door. He took the bag from her.

It all seemed so natural, so very right. He captured her mouth with a tender kiss, gentle yet filled with a promise of once again fulfilling her every desire and fantasy. As soon as his lips touched hers the moisture began to seep from between her pussy lips. Her insides quivered in anticipation. Her legs grew weak as they trembled in response to the excitement coursing through her veins. At that moment she wasn't sure she could even walk as far as the elevator. He gave her hand an intimate squeeze and they walked back to his suite.

He placed her overnight bag on the counter in his bathroom, then went to light the logs in the fireplace. She walked over to the glass wall and gazed out over the landscape. The outside security lights glistened off the snow. She looked up to the sky. The full moon shone through the breaks in the clouds. He had been right. Morning would bring blue sky and sunshine.

And the end to their idyllic hideaway.

If her thoughts had been confused earlier, she didn't know what to call them now. What had started as an intense physical attraction and the hottest sex on record had quickly turned into so much more...at least for her. But what about him?

Their interspersed conversations had not been anywhere near as awkward as she thought they would be. At times they had been far more comfortable than she wanted them to be. He had slowly, and it seemed unintentionally, allowed her glimpses behind the façade of the dynamic high-powered business executive who presented himself at the lodge a week ago. Insight into the man behind that public image. A look at the real person rather than the persona.

And she was growing very fond of that person. *Very* fond...if not more.

But what did he feel? What was going through his mind? She didn't know. Or perhaps she was afraid to find out.

The sounds of soft music reached her ears, then his voice. "A romantic fire, the full moon breaking through the clouds, some chilled champagne..." his words tickled across her ear as he wrapped his arms around her waist, "and a nice big bed. What could be more perfect?"

What, indeed? Her thoughts tried to wander, to find some type of foothold in reality, but the only reality she could find at the moment was the way Gage Brennan set her soul on fire and touched her heart. It was not what she wanted, but she did not have the ability to stop it.

He slipped his pajama top off her shoulders and down her arms until the garment fell to the floor then quickly doffed his pajama bottoms. Bare skin touched bare skin along the length of their torsos when he wrapped his arms around her. His rapidly growing erection reached up between them. Her breasts rose and fell with her ragged breathing. Her puckered nipples pressed against his chest. He ran his hands down the length of her back, then cupped her rear end in his hands and pulled her hips against his. She circled her arms around his neck.

Out of the corner of her eye, Afton saw a light

flash against the large bedroom window, then another flash. Her body stiffened and jerked to attention. A sense of urgency bordering on panic filled her voice.

"Did you see that? The two flashes of light? Is there someone out there? Can they see us?" She knew too many questions were coming out of her mouth all at once, but a feeling of anxiety had overtaken her common sense. She quickly withdrew from his embrace and grabbed the pajama top from the floor, pulling it on like a robe. The nervous tension churned in the pit of her stomach.

"It's okay. Don't worry. Probably just a couple of the lights downstairs burning out. It might even be one of the lobby lights. The lobby windows are about the location where the flash was." His voice was calm and soothing, but she could see the concern in his eyes.

"Maybe we...uh, maybe we should go downstairs—"

He placed his fingertips against her lips to still her words. "*We* aren't going to do anything. I'll go downstairs and check. I'm sure it's nothing serious. Even if someone could possibly be out and about, the doors of the lodge are locked and we certainly didn't hear enough glass shattering for someone to have broken in. I'll make a quick check of the perimeter just to confirm that it was nothing more than a couple of lights that burned out."

He pulled on a pair of sweatpants and a sweatshirt, stuck his feet into a pair of shoes and grabbed his master keys for the entire building and a flashlight. Pausing long enough to place a soft kiss on her lips, he extended a confident smile. "Wait here. I'll be right back."

Afton had been trying to assimilate what was happening and made a decision. "I'm going with you. Give me a minute to get dressed."

His smile faded, to be replaced by a stern expression. "No, I'd really prefer that you wait here."

A little shiver of apprehension darted through her body. She made eye contact with him and held it for several seconds. "Then you do think there's something wrong, don't you?"

"No, but that doesn't mean it wouldn't be prudent to be cautious. All I'm going to do is recheck all the doors leading outside to make sure they're secure. I'll check in with you from the hotel house phone at the registration desk before I come back upstairs."

He placed another tender kiss on her lips. "I'll be right back."

She watched from the loft as he left the suite. She heard the door click shut. A strange sense of loneliness settled over her. It wasn't fearful trepidation, but it certainly wasn't a calm sensation of well-being, either. She closed her eyes and tried to visualize where he was walking, the most direct route to check all the doors. He would have gotten to the lobby, checking the front entrance. She found herself nervously pacing back and forth.

Suddenly she turned and went to the master bathroom where he had placed her overnight bag. She dressed quickly. She didn't know what to expect but wanted to be ready for whatever might happen. The nervousness continued to churn inside her. She swallowed several times in an attempt to lessen the tightness in her throat and chest.

It seemed that he had been gone forever, but

glancing at the clock told her it had only been fifteen minutes. She kept glancing at the phone as if she could will it to ring so she could hear his voice saying he was at the registration desk and would be upstairs in a couple of minutes. But nothing happened. There was only silence.

****

Gage was pleased to find that the private entrance from the outside by his elevator was locked as it should be. It had been his first concern. He moved quietly on a circuit of the ground level—the lobby entrance, the outside entrance to the restaurant, the doors from the outside terraces. All were intact. The elevators from the parking garage beneath the building were shut down. The door to the stairs leading down to the parking garage was locked, too. He entered the kitchen, then came to an abrupt halt.

A quick adrenaline surge hit his bloodstream. His heart beat jumped up a level. The pantry door stood open, and the light shone from inside. He shined his flashlight toward the kitchen door that led outside. The floor inside the door was wet. His senses went on full alert. Someone had entered the building through that door. Then he heard the noise coming from the pantry, as if someone was going through the cupboards.

He glanced around, frantically seeking anything he could use as a weapon. His gaze fell on the large butcher knife. He grabbed it and took a calming breath in an attempt to slow down his pounding heart. He moved stealthily toward the pantry. Before he got half way across the kitchen, a large form of a man appeared in the pantry door.

It was a toss-up as to who was the most startled,

Gage or Stuart, the lodge's head chef.

"Holy shit, Gage. You just scared the hell out of me."

"You didn't do my nerves any good, either. What the fuck are you doing here? And just as important, *how* did you get here?" The street must be buried under maybe three feet of snow.

"I only live a couple of blocks away. Once the snow stopped, I strapped on the cross country skies and here I am. I've been concerned about the power and whether the refrigeration and freezers were working okay. There's thousands of dollars of food here, even more than normal because of the grand opening party. I wanted to see how much could be salvaged and start a damage assessment."

"At this time of night? Why didn't you just wait until morning? I'm sure the road crews will be working all night to get the main streets in passable condition."

"I wasn't doing anything else, and I was bored with television. What are you doing here?"

"I didn't make it out before they closed the airport. So I've been trapped…uh, along with Afton Pendleton."

Stuart cocked his head and raised a questioning eyebrow. "Just the two of you in the lodge all by yourselves? I'm surprised you're both still alive."

"Wipe that look off your face."

A soft laugh escaped Stuart's throat. "You misunderstood me. The way the two of you have been at each other's throat from the day you arrived, without someone to referee, I thought one of you would surely have killed the other."

"We agreed on a truce." He tried to suppress the

slight grin that tugged at the corners of his mouth. "And we haven't discussed or even mentioned the grand opening party plans. All and all, the time has passed pretty quickly."

"So you came down here to raid your kitchen?"

"No, it was a couple of flashes of light that made us wonder if someone was here. I was doing a security check of all the doors."

"That was probably me when I came in through the kitchen door. It could have been worse."

Gage couldn't stop the spontaneous laugh. "Yes, you could have set off the alarm and taken ten years off my life."

They talked for a couple more minutes before Gage started to leave. He turned back toward Stuart as he reached the door. "Give me a call on the house phone before you leave so I'll know that the place is empty again."

"Sure thing. I won't be much longer. So far everything appears to be in good shape except that it's cold in here."

"We never did lose power, but I turned down the heat to most of the building. I've got it set at fifty-five degrees. Definitely too cold, but warm enough that it shouldn't take too long to get all the rooms up to normal. I'll kick up the heat first thing in the morning. I imagine most of the local employees will be straggling in some time during the day so we can get organized again."

Stuart threw a sly look in Gage's direction. "I guess that means you and Afton will be on each other's nerves again as you gear up for the rescheduling of the grand opening."

Gage chose to ignore the comment, but Stuart's words continued to circulate through his mind as he climbed the stairs to his suite. So much had happened between them, things that could never be dismissed or relegated to the past. Would things change now that the circumstances would be returning to normal? And more important than that, exactly what was it that they had established? Hot sex certainly, but what else? There was definitely more, much more. They needed to talk seriously about what had happened and what it meant.

He unlocked the door to his suite and was immediately struck by the eerie quiet and total darkness. His heart beat a little faster as he reached for a light switch. Light flooded the room, but he didn't see Afton anywhere. He stepped inside and shut the door. Then it hit him. He was supposed to have called her before starting upstairs.

"Afton...it's me. Everything is okay."

He headed toward the stairs to the loft and the master bedroom. Half way up the stairs she appeared from his bedroom. He immediately noticed she had gotten dressed, as if she was about to leave. "Sorry I didn't call from the lobby. I already had the door unlocked before I remembered it."

"Did you find anything downstairs?" Her voice was less than firm.

He reached out for her hand, grasping it and pulling her toward him. "Yes, I found Stuart in the pantry. We scared the hell out of each other."

A quick look of relief settled across her features. "Well, I guess that solves the mystery."

The look of relief was quickly replaced by a hint of disappointment. "I guess that ends our privacy." A little sigh of resignation escaped her throat. "And it means I should return to my own room."

"Stuart won't be here very long. He said he was almost through."

"Even so, I'm sure there will be others coming back to work first thing in the morning. It wouldn't be good for anyone to know I spent tonight in your suite. In fact, it wouldn't be prudent for anyone to even suspect it."

He wrapped his arms around her. "I suppose you're right. And since it appears everything is about to return to normal, that means we'll be dealing with the grand opening party as the first item on our agenda."

"Yes, I suppose so."

He pulled her body tightly against his. "Do you think we can do it this time without all the arguments?"

"I don't know. I imagine it would depend on whether you allow me to do my job this time or insist on butting into the middle of everything again."

"I was hoping we could get through this without arguing."

"I was just hoping that we could get through it. But if you're going to—"

His mouth came down on hers, putting a stop to whatever she was going to say. He didn't want to be at odds with her. Quite the contrary. What he wanted was to be at one with her, his cock buried deep inside her pussy, their bodies moving together toward a repeat of the rapture they had already shared. He wanted to thoroughly explore every inch of her body again, to see the excited glow of orgasmic delight on her face, the passion burning deep in her eyes and knowing it was for him. Yes, they were definitely going to have to talk.

But not right now. Scooping her into his arms, he carried her into his bedroom and set her down on the edge of the bed. After kicking off his shoes, he leaned on the edge of the bed and captured her mouth with a kiss that quickly escalated.

Afton's pussy muscles clenched in anticipation and her heart pounded. It seemed that all he had to do was touch her and she instantly throbbed with a need she knew only he could fulfill.

The ringing of the house phone brought an abrupt halt to everything, allowing her a moment to catch her breath.

He grabbed the extension next to the bed. "Yes, Stuart." He listened for a moment. "Thanks. I'll see you tomorrow."

Gage returned his attention to Afton. "Now, where were we?"

She tugged down the front of his sweatpants, allowing his rigid cock to spring free. Leaning forward, she flicked the tip of her tongue across his cock head as she cradled his balls in her hand. After flashing a teasing grin, she licked her lips with a slow deliberate action. "I think we were about here."

The soft moan of pleasure that escaped from his throat was exactly what she wanted to hear. He was every bit as turned on as she was.

"Oh, yes." A husky rasp surrounded his words. "That's exactly where we were. I only have one suggestion."

She couldn't stop the sly grin that tugged at the corners of her mouth as she seductively ran her tongue across her upper lip again. "And what might that be?"

"That you get rid of all those nice clothes you

decided to put on while I was gone."

A tingle of excitement accompanied her words. "I will if you'll get rid of yours."

"You've got a deal."

Pieces of clothing quickly fell to the floor, then they snuggled into the king size bed. He teased her already puckered nipple with his tongue before sucking it into his mouth. Everything about her body excited him.

Gage's cock pulsed with need, but it was a need specifically for Afton Pendleton rather than sex just for the sake of whiling away the time by fucking a hot pussy. In fact, everything about her excited him. It was more than having his cock inside her, more than nibbling on her pussy lips and teasing her clit, more than the feel of her lips wrapped around his hard shaft.

It was so much more than merely the physical. But how much more and exactly what did that *more* consist of? He wasn't sure he was ready for the answer.

Her nipple popped out of his mouth. The wet, pebbled flesh glistened in the soft light like an exquisite jewel. He kissed his way down her body, tasting the essence of her creamy skin. He inhaled the aroma of her sex, the intoxicating scent shooting a tremor of excitement racing through his body. Her engorged little clit beckoned to him, and he responded by flicking his tongue across it several times before teasing the edge of her pussy lips.

Heightened anticipation shuddered through his body, accompanying the moment her hand caressed his balls. She gently nudged him to swing his leg across her body so that his hard cock bobbed in front of her face. And he gladly complied with her unspoken request.

A moment later, her soft lips formed a tight seal around his rigid shaft and her tongue laved across his cock head. Her moan of delight hummed along the entire length of his dick, sending waves of excitement through his body. Her mouth worked magic, a sensation he knew he would never get enough of. He sucked her clit into his mouth. Something else he knew he would never tire of.

Gage's heart pounded. Her mouth did fantastic things to his cock, too incredible for him to be able to maintain his control for much longer. He reluctantly withdrew his throbbing shaft from her mouth and rolled over onto his back. He grabbed the condom packet from the nightstand and handed it to her.

"Would you care to do the honors?" His words came out in a raspy whisper.

Afton straddled his body with her knees on each side of his thighs. She ripped open the packet and rolled the condom on his hard pole. He watched as her gaze swept up the length of his torso from his sheathed cock to his face where they held a hot second of eye contact.

He grasped her hips, lifted and slowly lowered her onto his cock. Ever so slowly he delved into the depths of her pussy tunnel. Once he was fully embedded inside her, she leaned forward and rubbed her clit against his pubic bone until she convulsed in orgasmic surrender. He bucked his hips upward, forcing her into a smoother rhythm. Her contractions continued to pull and tug at his shaft, propelling him toward his release.

She was so hot and so remarkable. He simply wasn't able to maintain his control as long as he wanted to. Hard spasms shuddered through his body. She fell forward into his arms. Her ragged breathing matched his as his chest heaved in an effort to catch his breath.

It had been one hell of a day, totally unexpected, yet one he knew would live in his memory forever. He held her tightly as he gently stroked her hair, reveling in the sensation of their naked bodies pressed together...bare skin touching bare skin the length of their torsos.

The morning would bring a return to reality. But would the light of day also bring an end of what had been rapidly developing between them?

Chapter Four

Afton stepped from her shower and grabbed the large bath towel. It was much later than she had wanted it to be. Spending the night alone in her own room had resulted in a restless sleep. It wasn't as if she and Gage had ever spent the entire night together before, where she was accustomed to having his body next to her as she slept. And the intimate personal time they had spent together could be measured in hours, not days. Yet that time had been so incredibly intense, filled with the maximum amount of togetherness possible. And it had been so much more than merely physical. At least it had for her.

But what about Gage? Had it been nothing more than a lucky interlude? A pleasurable way of passing the time until the weather cleared? As much as she had wanted to spend the night with him was equally as much as she knew she shouldn't.

Gage had walked her to her room after being unable to convince her to stay the rest of the night in his suite. When she had closed the door and stood all alone in her room, an incredible emptiness welled inside her. She immediately knew she was in over her head emotionally. She had wanted to run down the hallway after Gage and throw herself into his arms.

She quickly dried off and dressed for the day. The sound of machinery reached her ears. She peered out her window and saw four people working at clearing off the above ground parking lot and the walkways. One person was behind the wheel of the four-wheel drive vehicle with a snow plow scoop attached to the front and was being followed by someone with a snow blower. Two other people had snow blowers and were working on the walkways.

Afton allowed a little sigh of resignation, finished getting ready for a day of work, then left her room. She wasn't sure exactly what she would find downstairs, but she knew it wasn't what she wanted.

She took the stairs rather than the elevator. When she emerged into the lobby, she found a flurry of activity. Ronald Stevens, the lodge's manager, seemed to be having a meeting with the heads of the various departments...at least as many of them as could make it to work. The obvious exception was a missing Gage Brennan. Whereas it would be logical that the general manager would be holding the meeting with his employees, from what she had experienced of Gage during the days prior to the storm, he seemed to prefer being a hands-on owner. So, where was he?

A moment later, her question was answered when he strolled out of the office behind the registration desk. He had a computer printout in one hand and was talking on the cell phone in his other hand. Once again he appeared to be all business. He concluded his phone call and glanced around the lobby, taking in everything as his practiced gaze swept the area. A quick heated look passed between them when he spotted her, then he turned his attention to Ronald.

"The airport should be open in another two hours. We will have guests registering this afternoon so we have to be open for business and ready to provide guest services. I want the grand opening party rescheduled for next weekend. That means a lot of work to put everything in order."

"No problem, Gage. Basically everything is set. Naturally, Stuart will need to reorder some items and we'll have lots of phone calls to make along with getting ads in newspapers."

Gage gestured toward Afton. "Coordinate all your activities with our event planner. I'll be upstairs in my suite if anyone needs me. This little storm has put me way behind in dealing with some pressing business matters."

He had a couple more minutes of private conversation with Ronald, then disappeared behind the door marked private, leaving a somewhat stunned Afton staring after his retreating form.

Disappointment didn't begin to describe what crashed through her reality. Pain, hurt and despair came much closer. Had it all truly been nothing more than a temporary diversion for him? A game to pass the time?

She clenched her jaw into a hard line of determination. Well, if that's the way it was going to be, then at least he didn't string her along by making empty promises and allowing her to think they had something special. And if his hasty retreat to his suite was any indication, it looked as if he planned to stay out of her way. That would certainly make her job easier, and she had lots of work to do if she was going to pull this off by the weekend.

She tried to get her mind wrapped around a philosophical approach. She didn't have time to dwell on what might have been. He had taken her for a ride and now it was over. It wasn't like he left her empty-handed. It had been the hottest, most incredible sex of her life. That was something she would never forget.

She sucked in a deep breath, held it for several seconds, then slowly exhaled, followed by another steadying breath. Then she crossed the lobby toward Ronald. "I've put together a schedule for getting the grand opening back on track. I can take care of most of this myself from my room. It's going to involve a lot of telephone work. I'll use my room phone for outgoing calls and my cell phone for incoming ones so I won't be intruding into the hotel operator's time. I'm sure you have enough to do in rebooking rooms to accommodate the special invited guests."

A quick look of relief darted across Ronald's face. "Thanks, Afton. That will be very helpful." He glanced toward the door marked private before returning his attention to her. "I don't know what's with Gage this morning, but he seems quite preoccupied with something. That's not like him. He usually has all his priorities straight in his mind and can deal with a multitude of things at once. A very unusual and together man. Hmm…something is definitely bothering him this morning."

Afton returned to her room and settled into a busy work day. At noon she ordered lunch from room service and worked while she ate. As the day progressed, she began to relax a little…at least as far as work was concerned.

Everything was falling into place without any problems resulting from the last minute postponement of the grand opening celebration. She was thankful for the work load, something to keep her mind off Gage

Brennan and what might have been. Something to keep her from having to admit that her heart had been as involved as the rest of her.

Hot sex did not make a valid basis for a true relationship, but she had assumed there was more between them than just bare skin. She thought she had grown to know the man between the extremes. Could she have so badly misjudged the situation? Misjudged him?

Now she wasn't sure what to think or do. Of course, first and foremost was to maintain an outer show of professionalism in front of everyone, and that was best accomplished by keeping a safe distance from Gage. Her cell phone rang, interrupting her thoughts and jerking her back into the realm of the business at hand.

****

Gage stood just inside the door to his balcony. He stared out at the blue sky and sunny day. The new snow glistened across the mountains and on the trees. He could see the work crews plowing out the secondary roads now that the main ones were drivable. The town was coming alive again. He glanced up at the sound of a jet approaching the airport.

Excellent skiing on the three feet of fresh powder added to the existing base. What more could a ski resort ask for? He turned away, then slumped into the large chair in front of the fireplace. But what about the ski resort's owner? More than anything he had wanted Afton to spend the night with him. He liked the idea of waking up and knowing she would be there.

He understood the logic of why it was impractical under the circumstances. She was right. Stuart being in the kitchen signaled the reality that other employees would be at the lodge in the morning. The last thing he wanted to do was compromise her reputation, fuel speculation about what might have happened between them during the time everything was shut down or cause her embarrassment. He had been pleased with Stuart's assumption that they had probably spent the time trapped together by arguing.

But the night had felt so lonely. The sound of her voice, her laughter, the way she tilted her head...all the little nuances that reached inside him and touched his soul. He didn't know what to do. Explore the possibility of a relationship? Even though he had no emotional involvement in it, he was still legally bound to the last relationship he had tried—a relationship that had turned into a total disaster. It had been a long time since he had been as confused as he was at that moment.

What he wanted was tempered by his past experience.

He allowed a slight scowl to settle on his face. Exactly what was it that he wanted? He definitely wanted more of Afton Pendleton, but how much more? For how long? For what ultimate purpose? The questions frightened him, but the potential answers frightened him even more.

He pulled in a deep breath, held it for several seconds, then slowly exhaled. It did not provide him the release from the tension coursing through his body as he hoped it would. The ringing of the house phone broke into his thoughts. He stared at the phone as it rang two more times, then finally grabbed it from the cradle.

"Brennan."

The voice of Ronald Stevens greeted him. "Sorry to bother you, Gage. A reporter from the local newspaper just found out that the owner is on the premises and would like to do an interview with you. I have her on hold. Do you want to talk to her?"

"Sure, why not." He heard the lack of any enthusiasm in his own voice but didn't seem to be able to do anything about it. A moment later the reporter was on the line.

"Mr. Brennan? My name is Cynthia Hargrove. I'd like to bring a photographer with me and do an interview with you about the opening of the lodge. Is there any possibility we could do it this afternoon so it could make the morning's paper?"

Gage glanced at his watch. It was already two o'clock. "Be here in an hour."

"An hour? I had something closer to—"

"In an hour or not at all, Miss Hargrove." He couldn't keep the irritation out of his voice. "I have other obligations and that's the only time I can work you into my schedule. Perhaps if you had called earlier or would be satisfied with a time later this week..."

"Of course, Mr. Brennan. In an hour. Thank you."

A newspaper interview. He had no interest in the appointment he had just confirmed. Perhaps if it had been a national magazine he might have garnered more enthusiasm, but the local newspaper? Everyone in town already knew about the lodge, the natural hot springs, and everything else. A local interview would have no impact on business. And as far as news value, the storm was a much more viable story than yet another ski lodge. He glanced at his watch again and emitted a sigh of resignation. An hour. He had time to take care of some other business matters before being confronted by the reporter.

He forced himself out of the chair, ascended the stairs to the loft and sat at his desk. He had a mountain of paperwork having nothing to do with the lodge. He had been putting it off, and it wouldn't wait much longer. But before he got down to his own business, he grabbed the local phone book and made a quick call.

Gage kept busy until the phone rang and the desk clerk informed him that Cynthia Hargrove and her photographer had arrived for their appointment. He returned a couple of file folders to the desk drawer, then headed for the lobby. He glanced around before leaving his suite.

No, there wasn't any reason for the reporter and photographer to be in his private domain. He'd give them a tour of the guest common areas, show them a couple of guest rooms and answer their questions. With any luck, he would be sending them on their way in less than two hours. He wasn't too worried. She had mentioned needing to make a deadline for the morning's edition. It was a schedule she would have to follow.

He paused before entering the lobby, taking a minute to size up the reporter. She looked to be in her mid-twenties. The way she drummed her fingers on the registration desk while tapping her foot on the floor clearly defined her impatience. An immediate surge of caution made him wary and confirmed his phone call to the newspaper. Cynthia Hargrove was not a staff reporter. She was a freelance writer from whom they occasionally bought Sunday feature articles. She did not have a deadline to meet for getting an article in tomorrow's newspaper. His first impulse had been to cancel the interview, but instead he made another phone call.

He approached her and held out his hand. "Miss Hargrove? I'm Gage Brennan."

She shook his hand but held on to it a little longer than he thought necessary. "A real pleasure to meet you. May I call you Gage?"

"If you'd like."

"I really appreciate you taking this time for an interview." She flashed what she apparently felt was a sexy smile. "I've jotted down several questions, so shall we get started?"

Gage turned his attention to the man carrying a camera bag and holding a camera. "And you are the newspaper's photographer?" He turned a pointed look at Cynthia. "Perhaps you could introduce me to your associate?" He purposely allowed the edge to his voice. If she was running a scam or trying to make him believe she was an important publicity source, then she needed to sharpen her skills.

An obviously embarrassed Cynthia made the appropriate introductions.

"Why don't you ask your questions while I give you a brief tour of the facility?"

"Uh...yes, of course."

Gage took them through the lobby, into the great room with the large wood burning fireplace and comfortable chairs and tables for evening gatherings. He showed them the swimming pool and the pond fed by the natural hot springs. They toured the restaurant and cocktail lounge, then he showed them a typical standard guest room and one of the guest suites. He was fully aware that the photographer had not taken very many pictures and those he did take seemed to be more on impulse than something he had given any thought to or discussed with the reporter.

They finally returned to the lobby. "Well, Cynthia, I hope I've satisfactorily answered your questions. Now, if you'll excuse me."

"I do have another question, Gage. I've heard that you maintain a private owner's suite here at the lodge. May we see it? Get a taste of how the man who owns all this prefers to live?"

He cocked his head, made eye contact and leveled a serious look at her. "A private suite? And where would you have heard such a thing?"

"I...uh, I thought it was common knowledge." His question had obviously caught her off guard.

"In that case, it seems that *common knowledge* forgot to let me in on the secret. There isn't anything to show you that you haven't already seen." He extended his hand in a gesture of concluding their interview. "I look forward to reading your article in the morning paper."

He glanced toward the elevator just in time to see Afton step into the lobby. He quickly called to her and motioned for her to join them.

"Afton, this is Cynthia Hargrove. She's doing an article about the lodge for the local newspaper. Cynthia, this is Afton Pendleton. Afton is the event planner and is responsible for the grand opening party. This snow storm has made her work twice as difficult in that she had to gather up the pieces of the unexpected cancellation and try to redo everything in less than a week's time. I'm sure you'll find her input interesting.

So, if you ladies will excuse me, I have lots of work to do." He turned his attention to Afton. "Could I see you for just a moment?"

Gage led Afton out of hearing range from Cynthia. "I'm not sure what she's really doing here, but according to the local newspaper she doesn't work for them. The only thing she seemed interested in was questioning me about the existence of an owner's private suite, which I denied. It would seem to me that the angle for her story would be the last minute weather cancellation of the grand opening and then the scramble to reschedule it. So, perhaps woman to woman you could figure out what the hell she's doing here and what she's really after?"

Afton took a moment to assimilate his rapid fire comments. The wariness in his eyes matched the concern in his voice. And his nearness sent an emotionally charged shiver through her body. His aftershave combined with the masculine scent that was uniquely Gage Brennan. She wanted so much to be able to taste his lips on hers, to feel his arms around her. "I…you caught me at a loss. I was just taking a much needed break from my work. I guess I can give it a few minutes—"

"And then we need to talk. Just the two of us. We have things we need to get settled, things to work out. I'm not sure…" His voice trailed off as if he wasn't sure of what he wanted to say. "Have dinner with me in my suite. Is six o'clock okay for you?"

"Six o'clock will be fine."

"See you later." He flashed a sexy smile, but the intimate little squeeze he gave her hand said so much more. She watched his retreating form for a second as he headed toward the business office behind the registration desk. Then she turned toward Cynthia.

"What kind of information would you like? Do you have any questions about the grand opening celebration that I could answer for you?"

"Uh...well, not really. I think Gage provided all the information I need."

Afton shot Cynthia a curious look. "I've been reading the local newspaper every day since I arrived three weeks ago, and I don't recall ever seeing your byline. Which articles were yours?"

Cynthia's eyes narrowed as she stared at Afton. "I think I do have a question for you. What is your relationship with Gage Brennan?"

"My relationship with Gage? I'm an event planner. His company engaged my services to plan the grand opening party for the ski lodge."

"How long have you known him?"

"I met him for the first time when he arrived here a few days ago. Why do you ask?"

"Just curious. Tell me. What do you know about his business—the corporate structure? Does he have a staff public relations person or are you after that job?"

"You know what? I have a lot of work to do, and you don't seem to have any viable questions for me, so if you'll excuse me..."

It took all of Afton's effort to keep her irritation out of her voice. It had just become blatantly obvious that Cynthia Hargrove was looking for a job at the least. And at the most, she was after Gage himself.

A slight smile tried to tug at the corners of her mouth as she turned away from Cynthia. It was also blatantly obvious that whatever she wanted, she wasn't going to get it from Gage. He had disappeared as soon as he could get away from Cynthia. Or more accurately, as soon as he found someone he could hand Cynthia over to. She tried to stifle the amused chuckle that threatened to escape into the open.

Then her thoughts turned to more serious matters. Exactly what was it he wanted to talk to her about? Was dinner a way of softening the bad news that it had been nice, but now it was strictly business?

She had kept busy during the day while being secluded in her room. She had accomplished far more than she thought she would, especially considering that every time she paused, her thoughts immediately raced to Gage Brennan. Her body betrayed her at every turn. No matter how much she concentrated on business, she continued to crave his touch. The feel of his bare skin against hers. The taste of his kisses. His hard cock filling her pussy while she writhed in orgasmic abandon.

She took a calming breath as she glanced at her watch. She still had a lot of work to do before six o'clock. There were a surprising number of people checking into the lodge. In spite of the storm, it looked as if things were off to a good start. The grand opening party would be a week late, but she would make sure it was worth the wait. She took a few minutes to apprise Ronald Stevens of the situation with the *alleged* reporter, then returned to her room.

Afton worked until the time she needed to prepare for dinner. Following a quick shower, she dressed and applied fresh makeup then sprayed just a hint of her favorite perfume. She hurried from her room to his private elevator. A minute later, she stood in front of his door. She tried to swallow the anxiety that had been building inside her for the last five minutes. Raising her hand, she hesitated for a moment then knocked on the door of his suite.

The door opened, and he immediately pulled her into his arms, then shoved the door closed with his foot. It felt so good to be wrapped in his embrace again. Her body trembled with excitement. His mouth came down on hers, infusing her with all the passion that had previously passed between them. She opened her mouth and eagerly accepted his probing tongue as it brushed against hers. She ran her fingers through his thick hair, then wrapped her arms around his neck. Her breathing increased. Every fiber of her existence came alive with desire.

The sensual twining of tongues shot his pulse rate into high gear. Her taste exploded in his mouth. His cock throbbed with need—a need to be buried deep inside her pussy. His breath came in ragged gasps. He had to have her now.

His intention had been to sit down with her and figure out what each of them wanted, where they were headed as far as a relationship was concerned. But that would have to wait. The feel of her skin, the sound of her voice—it shoved his good intentions aside.

"We'll talk later." He didn't like the huskiness that clung to his words, but at the moment, he didn't have very much control over his all-consuming need for her. Just being near her brought out things in him he hadn't realized were there. Passion glowed in the depths of her eyes, robbing him of his last vestige of good intentions.

"Let's get out of these clothes."

"Yes."

Her breathless reply went straight to his cock as it strained against the front of his jeans, demanding to be let free. Clothes fell away. Gasps and moans of heavy breathing filled the air as they sank to the thick carpeting.

Gage pulled her on top of him as he stretched out, her wet sex tantalizingly close to his mouth. Moisture glistened on her pussy lips. Her engorged clit beckoned to him and he answered the call. A savory lick filled him with her unique spicing, a taste he'd craved every moment of the day.

Wrapping his arms around her hips, he kneaded the round globes of her perfect rear end. Just as he wiggled his tongue into her pussy and drew her clit into his mouth, her lips closed around his hard cock. A jolt of primal need shot through his body. He thrust his hips upward, wanting her to suck in more of his length.

He lost himself in the delicious feast she presented, drinking in her juices, teasing her clit and reveling in her earthy moans of delight. The marvelous things she was doing to his cock confirmed her level of arousal, one that matched his own. Two bodies perfectly attuned, each feeding the other's lustful needs. Excitement coursed hot through his veins. The churning in his balls let him know orgasmic release was only a moment away.

Disassociated considerations swirled through his mind, trying to grab his attention. Burying his cock deep inside her pussy, his condoms upstairs in the bedroom, pulling her off before he came in her mouth. All of it flew out of his head when her clit vibrated, her body shuddered and her pussy muscles grabbed at his tongue as the orgasm claimed her body. At that moment his only rational thought told him it was too late.

Hard spasms swept through him driving spurts of semen against her tongue. And still he continued to devour her taste, unable to relinquish the treat even in the throes of orgasm. It was only when she raised her head and his cock fell from her mouth that he was able to restore some composure. His chest heaved as he gasped for air.

He rolled to the side, repositioning himself so that he could take Afton is his arms. He held her body against his, smothering her face with kisses. Her tautly puckered nipples rubbed against his chest as she tried to slow her labored breathing.

The words started to form in his mouth, but he quickly buried his face in her hair to stop them. He had been only moments away from saying something he wasn't ready to say—telling her he just might be falling in love with her. He continued to enfold her in his arms until their breathing had returned to normal.

Hot sex on the floor only a few feet from the front entrance of his suite. He couldn't even wait to get upstairs. It screamed loud and clear that her mere presence literally robbed him of his restraint and composure.

Gage cradled her head against his shoulder. "As I said earlier, we need to talk." It all seemed so natural. Spontaneous sex followed by *business as usual* without any need to discuss it or explain it. Yes, it all seemed so natural...and comfortable.

He stood up, then assisted her. "Let's go upstairs."

They each picked up their clothes and walked hand-in-hand to his bedroom. Prior to her arrival, he had placed a bottle of chilled champagne in an ice bucket along with two champagne flutes. He uncorked the bottle, poured them each a glass and handed one to her. Neither of them made any attempt to get dressed.

"I know you've been busy and so have I, but I've really missed seeing you today. Before we move on to other matters, I want to explain that Cynthia thing. I'm sorry about dumping her on you. I had to get my distance but wasn't sure what to do. Then I saw you get off the elevator. I had complete faith in your ability to see through her charade and handle the situation without causing any problems or attracting undue attention."

A hint of surprise darted across her face. "Thank you for the compliment." It was quickly followed by a flush of embarrassment. "I should have known you couldn't be taken in that easily. If she's a reporter, then I'm a gourmet chef. It finally came down to her asking me if you had someone on your staff who did public relations and then *suggested* that perhaps I might be manipulating you in an attempt of snagging that job for myself. I'm not quite sure exactly what she was after. On the surface it appeared that she had used the reporter pretense merely as a means of hitting you up for a job, but I'm not so sure that was all there was to it."

"Pretending to want a job?" He tucked a loose tendril of hair behind her ear as he brushed a soft kiss across her lips. "Then that was ruse number two on her part. I did some phoning after agreeing to the interview. First thing I found out was that she doesn't work for the newspaper. The second thing I found out, after a little more digging, is that she works for my soon to be ex-wife's attorney. Apparently my attorney relayed what I said yesterday, and it spurred her attorney into action. I guess he sent Cynthia, or whatever her name really is, here to do a little snooping."

"I told Ronald she was a phony and asked him to keep his eye on her to make sure she didn't wander anywhere she wasn't supposed to even though I didn't know who she really was."

"Ronald called me a little while ago and said she finally left after hanging around the lobby for a while. Apparently she had asked him a couple of times if I was going to be coming back and he told her he didn't know my schedule."

Gage had done several things that afternoon in addition to checking out the journalism credentials of Cynthia Hargrove. And a lot of it had to do with his ever-increasing thoughts and growing emotional closeness to Afton.

And the more he thought, the more the confusion cleared. He didn't know if they really had anything together beyond torrid passion and hot sex, but he wanted to find out. He wanted to explore the possibility. And he couldn't seriously pursue her when he was still tied to another woman, even if they had been legally separated for three years and his only emotional ties to his wife were anger and frustration.

He built a fire in the fireplace, then they sat on the couch facing the flames. He put his arm around her shoulder and pulled her to him. An uncommon nervousness jittered inside him as he tried to gather the right words.

"I'm not sure how to say this. I've never had anything happen as quickly or hit me so hard as what happened between us. You said you wanted to know the man between the extremes. Well, what do you think? Is he someone you would want to spend a lot of time with?" He swallowed his anxiety but couldn't keep his dwindling confidence and uncertainty from showing in his voice. "Someone you think you might want to develop a true relationship with?"

The joy swelled inside her until she had a difficult time containing it. It wasn't at all what she had feared he might say but absolutely what she wanted to hear. "I think the man who exists between those extremes is someone very special, someone I definitely want to know much better."

The joy and overwhelming pleasure glowed in his eyes. "I've instructed my attorney to come to some sort of an arrangement with my ex so that she will truly be my ex-wife as soon as possible. I don't want to have to sneak around and wonder when the next situation like the pseudo reporter will present itself with my ex trying to pressure me by putting other people on the spot. I don't want her compromising your reputation, and the best way of preventing it is to finally dissolve the marriage—whatever it takes to do it."

His words had been the last thing she had expected to hear. She was almost afraid to say anything. "You did that for me?"

He brushed a quick yet emotion-laden kiss against her lips. "You never answered my question." A twinge of nervous energy shivered through him. Had she purposely avoided the question? "Do you think the man between those extremes is someone you want to spend a lot of time with? Someone with whom you could develop a true and lasting relationship?"

She leaned forward and returned his tender kiss along with a warm and loving smile. "Oh, yes. That man is precisely the person I want in my life."

He hadn't realized he had been holding his breath until he expelled it. The joy welled inside him. The look on her face perfectly reflected what he felt. He held her in his arms as they savored the quiet moments of emotional togetherness. He had never been happier than he was at that moment.

About the Author

Samantha Gentry currently lives in Kansas but has lived most of her life in the Los Angeles area.

For twenty years, she worked in television production before becoming a full time writer. For many years, photography was her avocation and that's what started her writing—non-fiction magazine articles to accompany her photographs. The writing eventually segued into fiction and novels.

Visit Samantha at
www.samanthagentry.com
http://samanthagentry.blogspot.com

To chat with Samantha Gentry and other Wild Rose Press authors of erotic romance, join us at www.groups.yahoo.com/group/thewilderroses.

Open In Private

by

Samantha Gentry

As a personal shopper, Charlene Vance values her professional association with longtime client Parker Simmons. But at the meeting to discuss the list for this year's Christmas purchases, she learns that Parker is divorced and the ex-wife is off his list. When lunch leads to dessert between the sheets, Charlene is eager to move their relationship beyond good business and incredible sex.

Parker Simmons doesn't want anything more permanent than what's on the menu for today. But Charlene's enthusiasm to experiment in bed satisfies his darker appetites and suddenly he's craving more. Parker might need her help with holiday gift ideas but he's got his own shopping agenda. On his list? Gifts only for Charlene—to open in private.

Thank you for purchasing
this Wild Rose Press, Inc. publication.
For other wonderful stories of erotic romance,
please visit our on-line bookstore at
www.thewilderroses.com.

For questions or more information
contact us at
info@thewildrosepress.com.

The Wild Rose Press, Inc.
www.thewilderroses.com